You Should Be
Mine

TOSHA COSTELLO

Disclaimer

CONTENTS

ACKNOWLEDGMENTS

Thank you to my husband and my son, I love you guys.
To my new readers, thank you for your support.

CHAPTER ONE

Lauren sat across from an empty chair as she sipped her wine. An empty chair that belong to her date Dewayne Vance. He said he needed to use the restroom and fifteen minutes later, there was still no Dewayne. They had been dating for a few months. They met at a club her and her sister decided to go to one night. Things didn't go as well that night, but a few days later he pleaded his case and she decided to give him another chance. He was a good guy that always knew how to make her laugh, but there were just some things that didn't add up and unfortunately, she didn't have any more time for his shenanigans.

She looked down at her watch as the minutes passed by and began tapping her fingers on the table, she was growing impatient. Another five minutes passed before she decided to get up and go see what was taking him so long. She made her way to a hall entrance. As she was about to turn the corner, she could hear his voice accompanied by a woman's voice. She stood there debating if she should say something or wait till later. She peeked around the corner and saw the two hugging. She decided not to say anything. He wasn't worth it or her time anymore, so she left instead.

Lauren walked gracefully to her car. She was pissed off, mostly at herself for giving him a second chance and for believing every word that he said.

"Lauren, wait!" Dewayne calls out as he ran towards Lauren.

She kept walking. She had given him many chances to come clean with whatever he was hiding, but he insisted on lying.

"Hey! I'm talking to you," he calls out. This time she stops and turns to him.

"Look I don't know what game you are playing, but I don't have time for them."

"What? I'm not playing any games."

"Oh really? Then who was the girl Dewayne?" she asked.

He stood there speechless. He had gone to the restroom and took forever coming back. Just as Lauren was about to go check on him, she sees him hugging someone else. She wouldn't have thought much of it, but the placement of his hands on the girl's ass gave him away.

"I'm waiting," she stated as she stood there with her arms crossed.

"She's just a friend Lauren. I had no idea she was

going to be here. I swear, I bumped into her as I was leaving the restroom," he said as he threw both of his hands up.

"Friends? Oh really? So, you hug all your friends by the ass?" she asked.

"I swear Lauren we are just friends. What more do you want me to say? What can I do to prove to you she's just a friend?" he begged.

"Umm…not a damn thing Dewayne, but please do me a favor. Why don't you add me to that friend list as well? Better yet, why don't you add me to the do not call friend list because I've had enough with everything," she said as she began walking away.

"What do you mean with everything? I have been nothing but nice to your ungrateful ass. No wonder you can't keep a man!" he yelled.

Lauren turned around with a grin on her face. This wasn't a laughing matter, but for him to call her ungrateful, and to say she couldn't keep a man… he just hit a nerve.

"Everything that I have, I worked hard for and I don't need some sorry ass man bringing me down."

He laughed at her words. "Sorry? Is that the way you see me? Some sorry ass man trying to bring you down?"

"What am I supposed to think? You won't tell me where you stay or work. Every time we go out, I have to end up paying!" she yelled. "So, excuse me for thinking so less of you."

"Maybe if you would have given up something, things would be different. I figured after ninety days you would come around and still nothing," he said as he held up his hands.

Lauren was disgusted as she stood across from Dewayne. "I'm leaving, and I suggest you do the same," she said as she opened her car door and got in. She left him standing there as she drove off. Maybe she was wrong for what she said to him. Sometimes she can be a little too harsh with her words, but she deserved better than what he was giving her. The fun times like late night talking on the phone, picnics, and walks in the park was all nice and dandy, but she needed someone with goals in life.

She and her sister didn't grow up poor. Her parents did ok in life. They worked hard together for everything that they had, and she wanted someone to do the same with. She was far from perfect, but she considered herself to be a great catch. She was educated, smart, funny at times and let's not forget beautiful. Medium complexion with shoulder length hair. Brown eyes and a smile that could light up the darkest room. She had a lot going on for herself. One day she hoped to have her own law firm, but in the meantime making partner at her job would be a great accomplishment.

Her ride home was quiet as she pulled up to her apartment. She gathered her purse and flip flops as she opened her car door and slid around in her seat. She then switched out her pumps for the flip-flops before exiting her car. She couldn't wait to get inside and relax. She had left work and came home to shower before heading back out for her date with Dewayne.

Once inside, she made her way to her bedroom, where she tossed her things aside and fell onto the bed. "Gosh tonight was terrible," she said out loud.

She knew it was late, but she needed to talk to her sister Layla. Since it was just the two of them, they were close. They told each other everything and always had each other's back, but lately, her sister hasn't been the same since falling in love. She spends most of her time with her new husband. They were expecting their first child. Everything happened so fast, but she was happy for her sister. Maybe one day she will have her happiness too.

Lauren got up off the bed and headed straight for the shower. She didn't bother to call her sister. She figured she would wait till the morning to tell her about her date from hell.

She entered the shower and placed her back against the wall. The water sparkled against her golden-brown skin and slowly cascaded from her breast to the floor. She turned around and let the water hit her back before turning back around and grabbing the shower head. She placed it gently over her womanhood, causing her to rest her back against the wall.

"Oh gosh," she moaned as her breathing deepened and began faster before bringing herself to pure pleasure. This wasn't how she imagined she would spend her nights, but it was certainly a good stress reliever for her. "I can't keep doing this," she said out loud as she hoped the neighbors didn't hear her.

She finished showering right as her phone began ringing. "Who is calling me this time of the night?" she thought to herself as she grabbed a towel off the towel rack and placed around her body. "I don't have time for this Dewayne," she said out loud.

She reached for her purse and retrieved her phone. Without even looking at the caller ID she immediately went off, letting Dewayne know how she felt.

"Look, Dewayne, do not call me anymore or text me. We are over with. There's no more us. Ok!" she yelled.

"Ok. I take that the date didn't go so well

11

tonight," said the caller.

"Layla?"

"Um yeah who else could it be?" she asked.

"Girl I'm so glad you called. I thought you were Dewayne. What are you doing up?"

"Well, I haven't heard from you. I wanted to make sure you were ok.," said Layla.

"I wanted to call you, but I figure you were sleep," Lauren replied.

"Seems like all I'm doing lately is sleeping. I had a meeting the other day and I swear I dozed off for a second," she laughed.

"I'm so happy for you. You seem so much happier since meeting Matthew. He's good for you, you're good for him," Lauren said with a smile. She then sat on the edge of her bed with her towel still around her, as she continued to talk to her sister. She was truly happy for her sister. Seeing her sister happy only made her realize how much fun love can be when you find the right person.

"Thanks, Sis. I am happy. Meeting Matthew wasn't part of the plan after breaking up with Tony, but I'm glad things happened the way they did," said Layla. "But enough of me. How was your date with Dewayne?"

"Well, let's just say that there will not be another date. I told him it was over."

"Ok, wow was it that bad?"

"Yesss. You are not going to believe what happened."

"I'm dying to know, so please do tell," said Layla.

"He goes to the bathroom and takes forever, and you know how I am," said Lauren.

"Please don't tell me you went into the men's restroom?"

"No, I didn't have a chance to. I saw his ass all hugged up with some female."

"What! Did you confront them?" Layla asked.

"I wanted to, but I just left instead. We never got a chance to order anything to eat and now I'm sitting here starving, hungry as hell."

"Lauren I'm sorry that this happened to you. Maybe they were just friends."

"That's what I thought until I seen his hands resting a little too low," Lauren said as she got up and put on a short black silk nightgown, followed by the matching robe. She then headed to the kitchen to look for something to eat.

"Ok yeah, he is a total loser."

"I know, and I wanted it to work out. He was nice and funny."

"If you like him that much just give him another

chance," said Layla.

"Girl no way. Don't you know, he is always broke as hell. I pretty much pay for everything when we go out. I don't get him sometimes. I always felt like he was hiding something," Lauren said as she had a seat on her living room sofa.

"Wait, you Lauren Hamilton have been paying for everything?" she asked. "Are you serious?"

"Yes, I'm dead serious. He even called me ungrateful. You of all people know I'm not ungrateful."

"You are definitely not ungrateful."

"Thank you!"

"But I must say, you do have high standards," Layla stated.

"There's nothing wrong with having high standards. If I didn't have high standards, that goofball would have moved in by now and try to talk me into giving up the cookies. I'm about to be thirty sis, I don't have time for games."

"Ok, what else are you holding out on? You two have been dating all this time and haven't had sex yet?" Layla said in a surprise tone. "You know what …I don't blame you. Look at how things ended."

"Maybe I should just keep to myself. This dating thing just isn't for me. Dewayne and I have been on and off and this time there's no getting back together."

"What about Matthew's friend Ron? He seemed like a nice guy. You two were getting along that day at the house."

"Ron," Lauren said with a smile. "He really is handsome that's for sure and smart, but we are too much alike. It would have never worked out between us."

"Lauren you don't know that. He's a good guy and you should give him a chance. Isn't that what you told me about Matthew?"

"Don't try to use my words against me," Lauren laughed. "It's not going to work out between Ron and I."

"You don't know this," Layla stated.

"I do. He told me so himself. He said he wasn't the marrying kind. I always thought I would be ok with not getting married, but after watching you and Matthew fall in love, I realized that I want that too," said Lauren.

For a few seconds, they both sat quietly on the phone. Lauren was reminiscing of Ron, while Layla's thoughts were of Matthew when they first met. The silence was broken by Layla's voice on the other end.

"Love is a beautiful thing when you have someone to share it with. I'm sure you will find someone that will love you unconditionally, but you need to be willing to accept it when it comes. Also, try not to be too headstrong." said Layla.

"Wait a minute, I'm the oldest here. I'm the one that gives the advice," Lauren said as they both laughed.

"What can I say, I learned from the best," Layla replied. "Well, I guess I will get some sleep and you need to do the same. And Lauren?"

"Yes, Layla."

"Give Ron a chance."

"On that note goodnight," Lauren said as they both hung up the phone.

Lauren remained seated on her sofa as she pondered on what her sister said about her being too headstrong. She was right, but that's just the way she is. Life experiences and learning so much along the way has taught her a great deal of things. Especially with relationships. That's why she had to keep her standards high. She wasn't looking to be any man's side piece. If any man wanted to be with her, they needed to have a plan and goals in life. They needed to be able to deal with her sassy ways because she wasn't planning on changing......not for him or anyone.

CHAPTER TWO

Lauren pulled up to her job at Watson & Associates. A law firm that she was proud to work at and was hoping to become a partner one day.

"Good morning Sunny," she said to the secretary on her way in to her office.

"Good morning Lauren. How was your date last night?" she asked as she came from around her desk and followed Lauren into her office.

"Sunny you know I don't kiss and tell," she said with a smile as she placed her things on her desk.

"Oh c'mon, just a little detail won't hurt."

"Just so you know, I'm only telling you this because there's nothing to tell," said Lauren.

"What? I'm so confused right about now."

"I broke up with him. So, as you can see, there's nothing to talk about," Lauren said as she went to have a seat.

"Wow, that bad huh?"

"Yes, and I don't regret my decision. I just don't understand men, especially Dewayne. He's so secretive and it drove me nuts."

"Girl, I know exactly what you mean. I was going through the same thing, with this guy I was dating," said Sunny as she took a seat. "I had to get rid of him right away. Trust me you made the right move."

"He was a really nice guy," Lauren said with a smile. "He's handsome, funny, but he's always broke." Her smile changed after that.

"Broke can't pay the bills and it definitely can't buy love either. Oh by the way, I made a fresh pot of coffee in the break room too."

"Thanks, well I need to get started on my day. I have a lot of catching up to do. Plus, I can't be discussing my love life at work."

"Girl we've been knowing each other for a while. Oh, I almost forgot," Sunny said before leaving out of Lauren's office and returning with a file. "Dale wanted me to give this to you."

"What is it?" Lauren asked as she took the file and began browsing through it. "It's a divorce case. He wants me to do this case alone?"

"I don't know. He just told me to make sure you got it."

"I'm already bombarded with so much already," Lauren said as she threw the file on her desk.

"Hey," Sunny said as she threw both of her hands

up. "I'm just the messenger and this messenger is headed back to her desk."

"Close the door on your way out please," Lauren calls out.

"Sure thing."

"Let the day begin," she said to herself.

As soon as the door closes, Lauren immediately began working, as she throws aside the file that was given to her. She figured she would get to it later. She needed to concentrate on what was already on her plate. She was still sleepy from last night. She needed that cup of coffee and needed it bad. She reached for her coffee cup out of her desk drawer and made her way to the breakroom.

"Seriously," she said out loud as she stared at the empty pot. Making another pot isn't what she wanted to do right now, but she had no choice. She began making another pot of coffee as her mind wandered back on last night's date with Dewayne. "Why can't she just meet someone nice," was the question that she always would ask herself. Someone that compliments her rather than complete her. She didn't need anyone to complete her, she was already completed. She just wanted a good man that can stand beside her. Her thoughts were interrupted by a male voice behind her.

"Good morning Lauren."

Lauren turns around to see her boss standing in the doorway of the breakroom. "Good morning Mr. Watson," she replied.

"Please call me Dale. How many times do I have to remind you?"

"Sorry Dale, it's just a professional habit."

"Did you get the file?" he asked as he stood there staring her up and down.

"Yeah, I did. I will add it to the list to do after I finish up the others. You know how I like to keep things in order," Lauren replied as she poured herself a cup of coffee. She could still feel Dales eyes on her, which was making her uncomfortable.

"I need you to make it top priority. It belongs to a close friend of mine. I promised her that I would expedite it."

"Oh…ok…that would have been great to know ahead of time."

"Well if you want me to assign it to someone else that can handle it, I can," he stated.

"No, it's fine. I can handle it," she said as she sipped from her cup. "If you will excuse me, I have tons of work to start on."

"You're excused," Dale replied as he watched Lauren walk away.

Lauren made it back to her desk wide awake. She reached for the file that she tossed aside earlier and began glancing through it.

"Let's see, what do we have here?" she said to herself as she studied the documents in front of her. "Evelyn V. Price. Fighting for the house, cars, business and trust fund. Sounds interesting."

Lauren studied the case until it was lunchtime. Busy days like this, she wished she would have brought her lunch. She spent her morning calling around and gathering information to present at pretrial. She still needed to contact her client and arrange a meeting. Should could ask Sunny, but she knows her plate is full as well. A knock came to the door and interrupted her thoughts.

"Hey girl, you got a minute?" Sunny asked.

Before she could say a word, Sunny was already having a seat in front of her desk. "Ok well, have a seat."

"Thanks," Sunny replied as she was already seated.

"Ok…what can I help you with Sunny?" Lauren asked.

"Who said I need any help with anything?" She said with a smile.

"Sunny, I have so much work to do. So, just spit it out."

"Ok, here goes. I wanted to know if I can leave

early. I know it's the middle of the week and we are busy, but I promise I won't ask again."

"You said that Monday."

"Well, today I mean it," Sunny replied with a sad puppy dog face.

"Doing that sad puppy dog face isn't going to work with me."

"It worked for Dale."

"I'm sure it did. He's a vampire looking for blood to suck. Be careful around him."

"What does that mean?"

Lauren said nothing but shook her head. "Nothing, anyway I'm assuming Dale said ok. Why are you asking me? He's the boss."

"He told me to make sure you didn't need my assistance with anything first and if it's ok with you I could leave. So, do you need my assistance with anything?" she said bubbly.

"As a matter of fact, I do," Lauren said while smiling.

"Seriously?"

"Yeah, I'm loaded with work. I need you to get these papers faxed to pretrial and schedule an appointment for Evelyn V. Price to stop by today or tomorrow," she said while handing Sunny a small stack of papers.

"Why are you doing this to me?"

"Doing what?" Lauren laughed. "What am I doing?"

"You're giving me work."

"Sunny you are at work still and that's why I'm giving you work. You haven't checked out yet. After you do those things, you can leave."

Sunny's face lit up with a smile. "You promise?"

"Yes, now go before I change my mind."

"Thank you! Lauren you are the best and I will make everything up tomorrow."

"Yeah, I know," Lauren replied as Sunny left out the door.

Sunny reminded Lauren of her younger sister Layla. She was fun, carefree and always smiling. Even through the mist of things she would still find the strength to somehow smile. Twenty minutes later Sunny stopped by Lauren's office to let her know she was leaving shortly and to also inform her that Evelyn was in the area and that she said she would stop by right away. Lauren was hoping that it would be later, but the sooner the better.

"Gosh I'm so hungry," she said out loud. She began searching for snacks in her drawer. "Yes!" She pulls out a cereal bar. It wasn't the best, but right now it will have to do. With three bites it was gone. She looked at the clock. It was almost two o'clock. The lunch crowd was probably gone, which meant the traffic should be light. "I can make it back in time."

"Ms. Hamilton," Cheryl said as her voice traveled across the phone speaker. She worked up front with Sunny and usually covers the front whenever Sunny is out and vice versa.

"Yes, Cheryl."

"Mrs. Price is here to see you."

"That was fast. I guess no lunch today," Lauren thought to herself. "Please send her back." Within a few seconds, a knock came to the door. "It's open," she calls out before the door opened. She looked up and sees Evelyn V. Price walking into her office. "Hello Mrs. Price," said Lauren as she came from around her desk and greeted her with a smile.

"How soon can I expect for this to be squared away?" asked Evelyn.

"Mrs. Price."

"Evelyn," she interrupted. "Evelyn is just fine. I'm not that old."

"Ok…Evelyn I just got the case this morning and I'm working on it as fast as I can. Before we get started I need you to sign this for me."

"What is this?" Evelyn said as she took the papers

that Lauren was holding and began reading them.

"It's a non-disclosure form. Basically, whatever we discuss in here, remains in here and cannot be shared. Doing so can hinder the case."

Evelyn looked from the papers to Lauren, as if she was deciding whether she should take her word or not. "Where should I sign?" she asked.

Lauren handed her a pen. "Sign and date here please," she said. "Also, here on the second page too."

Evelyn quickly signed and dated the documents and thrust the pen down on top of the papers, before sliding them back to Lauren.

"Everything's ok?" Lauren asked.

"Everything is fine. I just want everything to be over with as soon as possible."

"You can expect at least two months of wait time or at least one month at the most."

"I don't have two months of wait time. I need this to be completed ASAP. So, why don't you make those phone calls to speed up the process," she demanded.

"Evelyn, I don't know what Dale told you, but I can't snap my fingers and have all of this completed this week. It doesn't work that way. The system doesn't work that way." Lauren was losing her patience with this woman. She wasn't going to let some spoiled bimbo intimidate her by pushing her out of her professional zone and into the street zone. Because she had a street side to her and didn't mind showing it. "Why don't we focus on what we have in front of us. I read over the documents and it reads that you are requesting the house, the two cars, the business and a trust fund that is in your husband name."

"Our name. When we got married that trust fund became mine as well."

"I see. I'm assuming Mr. Price…."

"Vance," she said while interrupting Lauren.

"Excuse me," she replied.

"His last name is Vance. Dewayne Vance. Price is my maiden name. "

"I see," Lauren said as she sat there in disbelief. She knew it. She knew Dewayne was hiding something and finally, his dark secret has come to light. "Wow…ok."

"Also," Evelyn said as she reached into her purse and pulled out a large envelope. "Here's the bitch he cheated with," she said as she placed the envelope on the desk. "If I ever get my hands on her she's dead." Evelyn looked at Lauren and smile. "Our conversation is private right?"

"Right," said Lauren as she held the envelope in her hand. She was preparing herself for what she was about to see.

"Well, what are you waiting on? Open it up," Evelyn demanded.

Lauren was about to snap with all this demanding attitude coming from Evelyn. She could put up with bad attitudes, but she couldn't put up with someone who is not her boss telling her what to do. She doesn't take orders from anyone who doesn't sign her check. She didn't know what kind of game Evelyn is playing, but two can play this game. She looked directly into Evelyn's face as she opened the envelope. As she slowly pulled the photo out she glanced down.

"Oh, my goodness," she gasps as she placed her hand over her mouth.

"Exactly. I was the same way when I saw her. She's a child."

"She's definitely not a child, but certainly younger than you and me both," Lauren stated as she stared at the photos of Sunny and Dewayne. "Seems like your husband is good at living a double life."

"At least that's one thing we can agree on. I need to get going. Is there anything else that you need from me?"

"No, not that I can think of right this second."

"Please work on getting this resolved as soon as

possible," Evelyn stated as she walked to the door.

"Evelyn you know, there is one thing that I need. What is the name of the PI firm you used to have the photos taken?"

She reached into the outside pocket of her purse and pulled out a business card and handed it to Lauren. "If that's all. I will leave now and wait for your call." She turns and walks out the door.

Lauren studied the card and now had so much to think about. This wasn't going to be an easy case like she thought it was going to be. She needed to leave work early to get a head start on this case. She thought of sending Dale an email, but she decided to stop by his office instead. She gathered her things and locked her door to her office before making her way to Dale's office. She was about to knock until she heard a woman's voice coming from inside of his office. That voice wasn't any woman's voice it was Evelyn. She placed her ear close to the door. They were discussing the case along with something else. She couldn't quite hear everything, but she heard enough and didn't want to stick around.

"What in the hell is going on?" she thought to herself as she hurried away from the door. She went back to her office to leave a quick email before heading out again. "Cheryl, I'm leaving for today."

"Ok. Have a great day Ms. Hamilton," Cheryl replied as Lauren left.

Once she was in her Mercedes, she pulls out the card Evelyn gave her to look at the address. She knew exactly where this place was located and dreaded going there. It was where Ron worked. She has been avoiding him for the longest and now that the devil has showed up at her doorstep, she has no choice but to go. She resisted him all these months and today will be no different.

CHAPTER THREE

Twenty-five minutes later. Lauren pulls up at the Civic building. She took a minute to freshen up by reapplying her makeup and dabbing on her favorite perfume behind her ear and on her wrist. She gathered her thoughts before exiting the car and making her way inside.

"How are you doing lovely? You sho looking mighty fine there," A male voice said as she walked towards the elevators.

"Not today Larry," she replied as she got onto the elevator.

"Wait, how you know my name?" Larry asked as the doors to the elevator closed.

"Men," she said to herself as she watched the numbers light up on the panel. "This is why I am single."

The doors opened to the fifth floor and she stepped off. She looked around for the room number and realized the whole entire floor belonged to him. She was greeted by an older lady.

"You must be Lauren Hamilton?" Nancy asked as she came from around her desk and held out her hand.

"Yes, I am," Lauren said as she shook the lady's hand. "How did you know that?"

"Well, Mr. Avery said you were on your way up. I'm Nancy by the way. You can follow me. He said he was expecting you for some time now."

"Is that right?" Lauren found it odd that he was expecting her.

"So what kind of work do you do? Are you single too? Any children?" Nancy questioned.

"Whoa, alrighty then," Lauren laughed. "You are straight to the point I see."

"Honey, I am sixty-eight years old. I don't have time to sugar coat anything," she implied as they stood outside of Ron's door.

"Well, I guess you got a point there. Let's see I am a lawyer and I have no children. I am also..."

Her words were cut off as Ron's door opened. "Nancy will you hold all my calls please," he said as she stared at Lauren.

"Yes sir," she said as she went back up front to her desk.

"She a talker...really sweet, but a talker," Lauren said smiling. She hoped her cheeks weren't turning red because she was blushing.

"Yeah, I've been told that," he said as he held open the door for Lauren to come in.

"Wow, nice office and view."

"Definitely a nice view. I'm enjoying it," he stated as he stood behind her, resting his eyes on her physique.

"I now see how you saw me coming."

"Not yet, but I would love too," he replied.

Lauren turned around to face Ron with her cheeks on fire. "I was talking about the view."

"So was I. What brings you here today? Didn't think I would see you this soon."

"This soon?"

"Yeah. I mean, I knew it was just a matter of time before you changed your mind. Seeing you show up today is a surprise. You did turn me down."

"I turned you down because we wouldn't have worked out anyway."

"How did you figure that?"

"I just know ok. We're too much alike," she stated as he came closer.

"And what else?"

Ron loved a challenge and he loved the way Lauren was looking. Chasing a woman wasn't his style, but for some reason he wanted Lauren. His parents didn't have the best relationship and he said he would never fall in love, but ever since meeting Lauren, he had a change of heart.

"Plus, I was talking to someone at the time."

"But you're single now," he said as he came closer and stood directly in front of her.

"How do you know that?" she asked as her heart began beating faster.

"You must have forgotten the type of work I do. I'm the best at whatever I do," he whispered in her ear before looking her in the eyes.

Lauren tried her best to ignore the feeling that yearned for attention between her legs. He was so close that she could feel the bulge in his dress pants, pressing against her stomach. She could tell he was big and strong, which was making her wetter. Today was the wrong day to wear a skirt. It showed all her curves and apparently, he had no brakes.

"What else?" he asked.

"Um…I…" She couldn't get her words out. She tried to say something as his mouth captured hers. She wanted to pull back, but she needed this. Her arms went up around his neck and that was all he needed.

He pulled her close so that she could feel every inch of him, but he needed to be closer. His hand slid lower below her waist, gripping her ass as he pulled her even closer. He needed her to see and feel how hard she was making him and how bad he wanted her.

"I think we should stop," she said softly against

his lips.

"I think we should let our bodies do the talking."

"I'm serious Ron. We shouldn't be doing this at your job. Someone can walk in."

"No one ever comes in without knocking and plus I locked the door."

Right now, she needed strength. It's been a while since she's been with a man. Her heart was telling her no, but her body was saying something else. She was horny as hell and her body needed redemption. She loved the way she fit perfectly against his six-one masculine frame.

"I can't," she said as she pulled away. She needed to space between them to regain consciousness. She needed to think straight for what she was about to ask him. She needed answers.

"Water?" he asked as he took a bottle from his mini fridge.

"Thank you," she said as she took the bottle of water and turned it up.

"Thirsty?"

She only smiled, but it was soon gone as she got back into business mood. "Evelyn Price came to see me today and gave me these." She reached into her purse for the photos and handed them to Ron.

"Ok. They are photos my company took. What

about them?"

"How long did your company follow her husband around?"

"For a few months. Why? What are you getting at?"

"Ron, I'm sure you know who her husband was. Don't play with me."

Ron went to have a seat behind his desk. He reached into his drawer and pulled out a file. "Here," he said.

"What is it?"

"Just look inside," he stated.

She grabbed the file and opened it. Inside she saw pictures of herself and Dewayne. "I swear I had no idea he was married," she said as she took a seat in the empty chair facing Ron's desk. "I feel like a complete fool."

"Don't be. You had no idea. He was playing all three of you and I know you wouldn't have dated him if you knew he was married."

"How do you know that?"

"Because that's not you. You've built a name for yourself and I'm sure you wouldn't let some asshole bring you down."

"Thanks, Ron. I truly appreciate it. As you may already know, I stopped talking to Dewayne officially last night. We've been on and off for a while. I wouldn't even considered it as dating. We've only had a few dates here and there. I always felt like he was hiding something and now I know."

"You know how hard it was for me to sit back and let another man touch my woman and have you in ways I can't?"

"First of all, I'm not your woman and never was. Secondly, he's never touched me in any way like that. Hell, we've never had sex."

Saying that last sentence put a smile on Ron's face as he reached across his desk and grabbed Lauren's hand. "That means we have a chance?"

"A chance at what?"

"A chance at giving us a try. We are right for each other," said Ron as he leaned in and gave Lauren's hand a kiss. The sound of Lauren's stomach caused them both to laugh.

"I'm so sorry. I haven't eaten today. I've been so busy with this case, I didn't have a chance to get lunch."

"How about we have dinner later? Don't tell me you're not hungry because we both know you are," Ron said as he crossed his arms.

He was right, she was hungry as hell and right about now, he was looking temptingly good. "Ok, what time should we meet up and where bout?"

"I'm not Dewayne. I will pick you up at around seven."

"That's two hours from now."

"Then I suggest that you get a head start. You can always shower here," he said with a smile.

"No thanks," Lauren replied as she fixed her hair and makeup, as well as her clothes. "I need to get going. I will see you later." She could feel his eyes undressing her as she left out of his office.

"Honey, your skirt is twisted," Nancy said as Lauren passed by her desk.

She was slightly embarrassed. She couldn't help but smile. "Thank you, Nancy." Once inside the elevator, she took that moment to fix her skirt and blouse again before heading to her car.

Her drive home was filled with smiles. Sometimes she would call her mom or sister on the way home, even though they both hated being on the speaker. She just thought it was safer that way.

As soon as she got home she hurried and jumped in the shower. She needed to be quick. Knowing Ron, he would surprise her and show up early with an appetite for something else. Her body relaxed as soon as it felt the water. She spent another ten minutes in the shower before drying off and walking to her closet.

"Let's see, what can I wear?" she thought out loud. She decided to go for the olive color off the shoulder midi dress with elbow length sleeves and her nude strappy heels. She dressed and stood in front of the mirror, examining herself from head to toe. She loved the way the dress accentuated her curves, which caused her to smile at her reflection. She wondered if wearing a dress was the wrong idea. After all, this was just a simple dinner date. She searched for a change of clothes just as her phone rang.

"Hello?"

"Hey, Sis! Please tell me it's true!" Layla said with joy.

"What are you talking about?"

"Your date with Ron!" she yelled. "I'm so happy for you too. I know you would come around and give him a chance, he's a nice guy!"

"Whoa, slow your horses. It's just a simple dinner date."

"Um yeah, sure it is. Are you dressed already?" Layla asked.

"Yeah of course."

"Is it a dress?"

"Yes, Layla!"

"Is it clingy?"

"Layla, what are you hinting at?"

"Just answer the question. You're under oath," said Layla as they both laughed.

"Yes, it's clingy. There's nothing wrong with a little clinginess," said Lauren.

"Final question. Are you wearing stilettos?"

"Oh, my goodness," Lauren laughed. "Yes, I'm wearing stilettos. That doesn't mean anything. You want to know the colors of my shoes too?" she joked.

"Why would I want to know the color?" Layla replied.

"It's official, you are the crazy one," Lauren said jokingly.

"No, the only thing that's official is you and Ron. You wore a dress for easy access and once the dress comes off, the heels will drive him crazy."

"You're reading too much into this little date and how do you know we were going out?" Lauren asked curiously.

"Well…."

"Hold that thought. I think he's here," said Lauren. "We are going to finish this conversation later. I have to go bye," she whispered as she hung up the phone. She took one another look in the mirror. Thanks to her sister interrupting her, she still had the dress on and there was no time to change. She did one final glance in the mirror before making her way to the door. She smoothed out any wrinkles she had and ran her fingers through her hair. She took a deep breath and opened the door.

"Dewayne?"

CHAPTER FOUR

Lauren stood in the doorway, while slightly holding open the door. "What are you doing here Dewayne?" she asked.

"Wow, you look amazing. Then again you always look amazing."

"What do you want?" she asked again.

"I just need to talk to you about last night. Maybe we can work things out?"

"I'm not the one you should be working things out with. For starters, try your wife because we have nothing to say to each other."

Dewayne stood there staring at the floor before looking at Lauren. "So...you know?"

"Yeah, of course, I know and I'm representing her

in her divorce case. So, can you please leave now?"

"Lauren please just hear me out," he begged. "It's not what you think."

"I don't need a low life, two-faced unfaithful wannabe bringing me down. I asked you nicely to leave. Don't make me call the cops," said Lauren, but he didn't budge.

He stood there like he still had something to say and he did. "I'm tired of you talking to me like I'm some kind of chump," he said with anger. "You better watch who you talking to. I'm not your child."

Lauren already saw where this was going. She didn't have to entertain this fool. "Goodbye Dewayne," she said as she intended to close the door but was stopped when he placed his foot in the door.

"Dewayne get away from my door, now!" she demanded. She tried her best to keep her voice down, so she wouldn't cause a scene.

"Or what?" Dewayne said as he placed his hand on the door.

"Or you might find yourself in jail. Better yet, in a

body bag or buried alive," Ron said as he was walking up to Lauren's apartment.

"Who in the fuck are you?" Dewayne asked as he turned towards Ron.

"You're worst enemy if you don't step away from that door," he said as he went to stand in front of the door. He placed his body between Lauren and Dewayne. "Are you ok?" he asked Lauren.

"I'm ok. Dewayne was just leaving," she stated as she stared at Dewayne with a slight smile on her face. For the first time in a while, she felt like she was floating on cloud nine. Standing up to Dewayne only made her even more attracted to Ron. No one has ever done such a thing for her. She's usually the one standing up for people. She did the protecting and now it seems as if she might have her own protector.

Dewayne stared at Lauren with rage in his eyes before walking away. She could tell, it wasn't over. She's never seen him this way, but there's a first for everything.

"Are you sure you're ok?" Ron asked again.

"Yeah, I'm ok. What's in the brown bag?"

"A little something for later," he stated as he handed it to her. "Just make sure you put it in the freezer."

"Ok, I'm anxious to know what it is," she said with a smile as she placed the bag in the freezer.

"Are you ready?" he asked.

"Yeah, I just need to grab my purse."

"Ok," said Ron as he had a seat on the sofa. "You have a nice place here."

"Thanks. I'm ready if you are."

He stood up and looked at Lauren. This was his first time tonight taking in her beauty. "Did I mention how beautiful you look tonight?" he said as he gently kissed her lips.

She couldn't hide the fact that she was blushing. He knew what he was doing, and it was working. "Thanks, you cleaned up well yourself." She was hot and needed air. If they kept this up they would have to skip straight to dessert. "I think we should get going."

"I think you're right."

Lauren locked her door as they made their way to

his SUV. He helped her in first before taking his seat on the driver side.

Fifteen minutes later they pulled up at a seafood restaurant. "I hope you don't mind me picking out the restaurant."

"No, it's fine. I can eat just about anything right now."

He got out and opened her door. She could get used to this. So far, he has proven that chivalry wasn't dead. The night could only get better.

"Oh my goodness, do you see the line?"

"Yeah, this place is always packed. You will love the food," he said as grabbed her waist and pulled her close and they began walking towards the entrance. She expected them to wait in line, but they were escorted immediately inside to a private booth. Lauren entered one side and he sat right beside her. The waiter soon came and took their drink orders.

"This is nice. I've never been here before," said Lauren. "I actually don't get out much."

"Maybe we can change that. So, tell me, what's

going on with you and this Dewayne?"

"There's nothing going on. The doorbell rang, and I opened it. I would have never opened the door if I had known it was him," she said as she sipped her wine.

"Did he say what he wanted?"

"No. I didn't give him a chance to. I'm representing his wife. I don't need to be talking to him until the case is over, due to conflict of interest. But there's something that puzzles me, that I can't quite figure out yet."

"You mind sharing it with me?"

"Well I suppose I could give you the part that's not in the non-disclosure agreement," said Lauren as the waiter came and took their orders. "Before I came to see you, I went to my boss office to let him know I was leaving. Right as I got ready to knock, I heard him and Evelyn talking about the case. I heard her say that she needed out before five years is up."

"Maybe he's looking out for Evelyn."

"Maybe, but something doesn't seem right. I don't know what it is, but I trust this gut feeling that I have. I think she's not telling me everything, but why.   I'm her lawyer."

"I'm sure you will figure this out. Just be careful," he said as the waiter brought them their orders and refilled their glasses. "Divorce cases can get messy and dangerous. Sometimes they are worse than a criminal case."

"Yeah, you're right, because you know what you are walking into when it comes to a criminal case. While with a divorce case you don't," Lauren said as she ate her food.

"Exactly. I hope you are enjoying your food."

"I am. Thanks again for inviting me."

"Thanks for accepting the invite," said Ron.

They both laugh as they ate their dinner. For the first time, Lauren couldn't help but to notice how funny and handsome Ron was, while he couldn't help but to take in all of Lauren's beauty. She was simply gorgeous, and he wanted more than just her body. He wanted all of her.

He just needed to prove to her that he isn't the man that she met months ago. The man that never wanted to settle down because he didn't want to end up in a struggling marriage like his parents. His father cheated on his mother. He saw the affects it caused and vow to never settle down. He didn't want to cause the same pain to anyone, but now he wanted to love and the only person that was a match, was Lauren. At thirty-five, he was ready to share his life with her and her only. Somewhere in the beginning, she somehow made her way into his heart. Now his heart can't beat without her.

"How about we leave here and go open that package," he stated with a smile.

"Sounds great. I'm dying to know what it is," she replied as they exited their booth and drove back to her place.

"Thank you again for tonight," Lauren said as she unlocked her door. "I had a great time."

"Me too. You know you should really look into getting a peephole in your door," said Ron as he closed the door behind him.

"I know. I just never got around to it. Can I get you anything to drink?"

"Just water will do," he replied as Lauren went to get him and her a bottle of water.

"Here you go."

"Thank you lovely."

"Apparently you know how to soften a girl's heart," she joked.

"Oh, is that what you think I'm doing, softening your heart?"

"I don't know, you tell me."

"Maybe…maybe not," he said as he moved closer.

"Maybe I need to try to soften your heart a little," she replied.

"Baby, there's nothing soft on me. At least not right now."

She was totally in blush zone. It was written all over her face again. She was trying her best to ignore the feeling that was being created by him. His touch, the smell of his cologne and his smile were all driving her body insanely crazy. Again, he was enjoying this. Maybe a little too much.

"You know what? I almost forgot about the freezer. How about we go take a look inside that bag?" she said as she went to the freezer. He followed behind her.

"I hope you like it."

"We shall see," Lauren replied as she opened the bag. "Oh, my goodness. How did you get this? This place never has my favorite flavor on hand and you were able to get it."

He smiled. "I have my ways."

"How did you know that butter pecan was one of my favorites? You had help. I know you did." She reached for two bowls and spoons.

"I had help from you. I remembered you mentioning it at your sister's wedding."

"You have a great memory."

"I suppose, but some things are hard to forget. Especially when they remind you of someone special. How about you grab a bowl and I'll feed you."

"So, you're going to make me eat alone?"

"Absolutely not. I'm going to join you in more than one way," he said as Lauren followed him back to the sofa. He then took the bowl from her and began feeding her. "How about for every drop that misses your mouth, I get to lick it off?"

"Well I guess I better make sure to eat every drop," she replied.

The first scoop he places against her lips before she opened her mouth. So far everything was going great until he got to the third scoop.

"Looks like you have some on your lips," said Ron as he leans over and kissed her lips gently, pulls back and looks into her eyes.

"I think I want a little more," she replied. She knew where this was going to lead them, but she didn't care because she wanted to go.

"Whatever the lady wants, the lady gets," he implies as he places a generous amount of gelato on the spoon. The spoon was so overloaded that some fell onto her chest and began melting. "I better get that," he said as he placed the bowl down and did just that. His mouth came down on her chest. He began tracing his tongue over the melted cream. All the way down to the top of her right breast. He takes his hand and slowly pulled down the fabric, revealing her right breast. He needed a taste and a taste is what he got as he took her perky nipple into his mouth and started sucking and licking. Rolling his tongue around it as she moved against his mouth. He then kissed his way over to her left breast and again removed the fabric revealing her nipple. He wasted no time in devouring it.

Lauren's body was on fire and she was a complete meltdown. She needed out of her clothes right away. There was too much fabric between them, keeping their bodies apart. She slid her arms out of her dress and let it rest around her waist, giving him partial excess of what's to come. He grabs the hem of his shirt and pulls it over his head, now giving her a partial view of what she was getting into. He pulls her close and they began kissing, only coming up for a breather. They were both trying to catch their breath.

"Bedroom?" he whispered softly against her lips.

She shook her head in agreeance. "Yeah."

He scooped her up in his arms and carried her to her bedroom, where he stood her up on her feet. He kissed her again before sliding her dress all the way down, causing it to nestle around her feet. He stood back to take in the beautiful sight he was seeing as Lauren walked seductively to him.

She rested her hand on his belt buckle and began working her fingers until it was loose. She wasted no time in undoing the button on his pants, followed by the sweet sound of the zipper. She took a deep breath when she saw the print of him bulging against his boxer briefs.

He could feel her staring at him, which was causing him to grow even harder. He bent down and took her lips again. While still kissing, he grabbed her and lifted her up so that her legs could wrap his waist. He hurried to the bed, where they both fell, with him on top. He stopped to slide her panties off as he did the same. He reached into his pants pocket and pulls out the one thing that would be between them, before settling back into position. He placed himself at her center and looked into her eyes as he plunged into her.

She knew he was big, but her guestimate was wrong as ever. He was much bigger than she imagined, and he wasn't holding back. He was filling her up with every inch of him, causing her to lose control. It's been a long time since she's been with anyone and it showed. She tried her best, but she couldn't hold on any longer. Her body began to tremble as he pumped faster and harder,

harder and faster. Until they both came.

"This was just a sample. There's more where that came from," Ron said as he stayed inside of her, making himself right at home.

CHAPTER FIVE

The alarm clock sounded, waking Lauren as she laid sprawled out on her queen size bed. Her body was sore after two sessions of lovemaking with Ron. She rolled over hoping to be wrapped in his arm, but instead, she felt an empty space. She raised up and looked around the room.

"Ron?" she called out in her morning voice, but there was no answer. She slipped on her black silk robe and made her way down the hallway where she could smell the aroma of coffee coming from the kitchen. "Ron," she called out again.

"Out here," he replied as he opened the front door.

"What are you doing?" she asked.

"Installing you a peephole. I hope I didn't wake you."

"No, actually I didn't know you were gone. You

know I could have gotten that taken care of."

"Yeah, I know," he said with a smile.

"Thanks for making coffee too. Seems like you've been quite busy this morning," Lauren said as she made herself a cup of coffee.

"Not as busy as I would have like to have been," said Ron as he closed the door. He then made his way to Lauren and gave her a short kiss on her lips. "I need to get to work early."

"Yeah, you and me both. I need to get a head start on this case. Hopefully, I won't have to contact Evelyn today. She seems like a real bitch and I have to bite my tongue to keep from saying exactly how I feel." She took another sip from her coffee. "I guess I shouldn't have said that about my client."

"She can be a real pain in the ass, but don't let her take you out of your professional zone. Don't fret, it'll be over soon."

"You're right."

"Well, I need to get going. Maybe we can catch lunch later?"

"Yeah maybe. Thanks again for the coffee and the peephole," she said with a smile as she followed Ron to the door.

"No problem. If you need anything call me," he stated as he gave her a kiss then left.

Lauren then closed the door and locked it. She then rested her back against the door. Her heart was beating with joy as she stood there blushing and smiling like a teenager in love.

"Snap out of it," she said to herself. "He's probably no different from other guys."

Lauren carried on with her morning. A cup of coffee, then shower, get dressed and a cup of coffee to go. She checked her phone, no call from her sister. "If I can't sleep in you can't either," she stated as she began calling her sister's number. Right as she started to hang up, the phone was answered.

"Yes?" said Layla.

"Well good morning to you too. How are you feeling?"

"So, so. I couldn't sleep last night. Matthew wants me to stay home today. He said I'm working too hard."

"Layla, he's right. You have been working long hours. You need to take it easy, you have a little one to think about now," said Lauren as she grabbed her briefcase and headed out the door.

"I know, but you know I hate just sitting around the house doing nothing."

"All I can say is, you better get used to it now because when the baby comes you're going to be wishing for a nap," said Lauren as she walked to her car. "Layla I'm going to call you when I get to work."

"Why? You call me and wake me up and now you can't talk," Layla joked.

"I'm about to drive, safety first."

"Seriously?" said Layla.

"Yes seriously," Lauren said as she drove off. "I would put you on speaker phone, but I know how you hate……." she said as her voice drifted off. She made a left turn and looked up into her rearview mirror. A white truck seemed to be following her, but she wasn't for sure, so she made another left turn. The truck kept its distance but remained behind her.

"The speakerphone? Yeah, I hate it so don't put me on it. Hello? What are you doing? Lauren?" asked Layla.

"Yeah, I'm here," she replied. After making a third left, she looked up again and the truck was gone. "Just thought I saw something," she said as she placed Layla on speakerphone. Maybe it was just a coincidence.

"I know you just placed me on speaker phone because I can hear an echo."

"Sorry sis, but why have a perfect speakerphone system in your car if you can't use it?"

"I…don't…know, but what I do know is, I am going back to bed."

"It's good to know you are listening to your husband's advice and taking it easy."

"He's in bed. That's the only reason why I am going back to bed," she said as she laughed. "Wifey duty calls."

"Ok, yeah on that note I'm saying goodbye," Lauren said as she laughed before hanging up.

Her short commute to work seemed longer due to the thought of being followed. She pulled up at her job and dreaded going in to work on the case. This was her first divorce case. She knew that this case was going to be different from the other cases she had been working on, but she had no idea that it would be this difficult. Maybe if she'd had more time the stress toll wouldn't have jumped in so soon.

"Good morning Ms. Hamilton," Sunny calls out.

"Good morning Sunny. How many times do I have to say no Ms.? Just Lauren will do."

"I know, I know it makes you feel old. There's nothing wrong with growing old," she joked. Sunny was always smiling. She loved to joke a lot. Sometimes it was hard to tell if she was being serious or not.

"We're almost the same age Sunny."

"Shut your mouth. Are you sure? Because you act way older than me. Like super older."

"You and your jokes. I hope that joke works for you when you're trying to leave early again," she said with a laugh.

"Ok nice comeback, not funny, but a good comeback."

Lauren entered her office and immediately began working. She opened the file that was given to her yesterday and began reading over the documents. Something just didn't feel right.

"What is really going on?" she said to herself as she read the small print on the Trust, but soon was interrupted by a knock at the door. "Come in," she called out.

The door opened and in walks Dale. "Good morning Lauren."

"Good morning Dale," she replied as she continued working.

"How's the case going? Were you able to get everything squared away?" he asked as he sipped his coffee from his insulated tumbler cup. He then took a seat in front of her desk and placed one leg over the other.

"Dale, I've only had the case for one day. I'm not superwoman you know. This isn't going to be the simple case. I know you wanted me to put a rush on things, but I can't. I just can't. I don't want to rush things and screw up," she said as she continued working. "You of all people should know that a divorce case takes more than a day to complete. Why all the rush anyway?"

"I told you, Evelyn is a good friend of mine. I promised her that we will make sure everything is taken care of as soon as possible and in a timely matter."

"But why the rush?" she asked again.

"That's for me to know and for you to find out," he replied as he got up from his seat and made his way to the door.

"What does that mean?"

"It means some things are better left untold. So, if you want to become partner here, do your job without questions," he stated before leaving.

Lauren sat there thinking about what Dale had just said. So many questions. Why the rush? And what were they hiding? Somehow, she felt like Dale knew more about her case than she did. Three hours into work she was finally making progress. She now knew why Evelyn wanted to speed up the process.

"Knock, knock," said Sunny as she peaked in Lauren's office.

"Yes Sunny," said Lauren.

"What are you doing for lunch?" Sunny asked.

"I brought a simple salad for lunch."

"Um. what is a simple salad."

"You know, lettuce, cheese, and baby tomatoes."

"Lauren, that is not simple. That is ridiculous. Where's the meat?"

"I ate a heavy meal last night. So, today I am

trying to eat a little healthier."

"I'm going to get a nice juicy loaded burger with fries and a diet coke," said Sunny. Which caused Lauren to laugh.

"A diet coke?"

"Hey, you're not the only one trying to watch her weight," she laughed. "Well, I'm about to step out to get lunch. I'll wait a few minutes, just in case you changed your mind."

"Ok. Hey Sunny," she calls out before Sunny turned away.

Sunny peeped her head in the doorway "Changed your mind already?"

"Um, no. Could you come have a seat please?"

"Oh, this must be serious," said Sunny with a smile as she took a seat. "Ok, talk to me. What's going on?"

"Evelyn Price showed up yesterday and brought a surprise with her." Lauren reached into the file on her desk and pulled out some photos and handed them to Sunny.

Sunny looked at the photo and suddenly her smile vanished. "He was married? He never said he was married. I even asked him," she explained as she looked up at Lauren. "I would never date a married man Lauren, I had no idea. I swear."

"I know. Trust me I know. Remember the guy I told you I broke up with?"

"Yeah what about him?"

"Well, he's the same guy you were dating. I also had no idea he was married or seeing you," said Lauren.

"Oh gosh, what a fucking jerk. Apparently, he must have been playing both of us. No wonder he never visited me at work. He knew you worked here too," said Sunny.

"I always thought he was hiding something. He didn't want me to know where he worked or lived. The night I broke up with him, I saw him all hugged up with some woman. I took that as my hint to leave him alone. I'm glad I did," said Lauren as she stared at the file in front of her.

"What was Ms. Price wearing yesterday?" asked Sunny.

"Um……she was wearing white trouser pants, with a blue and white off-shoulder shirt, with red heels. Why? What does that have to do with any of this?"

"Lauren, we walked right past each other yesterday while I was leaving out. "

"Are you sure?"

"Yes, I'm sure. Why didn't she say anything to me yesterday?"

"I don't know. Maybe she didn't recognize you?" Lauren thought that was strange.

"Yeah, maybe."

Lauren began wondering, why didn't Evelyn say anything to Sunny? If she was in Evelyn's shoes, she would have confronted the woman who her husband cheated with. Everyone is different she guessed.

"Well I'm going to try to get some lunch," said Sunny as she got up from her chair. "And try to eat."

"Sunny, I'm really sorry for spoiling your day. I just thought you should know."

"You didn't ruin my day. I just hate to think that I'm the reason why a marriage is broken," said Sunny.

"You're not the reason, he is. He knew he was married. He should have said something. So, don't beat yourself up over this. Now go get yourself that big ass juicy burger," she said with a laugh right as her cell phone began ringing.

"Ok well, if you need me call my cell."

"I will and Sunny….be careful."

Sunny smiled as she closed the door and headed out for lunch., leaving Lauren to continue putting together pieces. She looked down at her cell phone and saw a missed call from Ron. She should call him back, but she didn't want to seem like she was waiting for his call. So, she decided to wait a few minutes instead. Meanwhile, she had work to do, phone calls to make and a judge to see.

CHAPTER SIX

Ron stared at his phone as he tapped his ink pen against his desk. He hasn't heard from her all day. His mind then went back to his date with Lauren. She was incredible, smart, and beautiful. He needed to spend more time with her to show her, that he wasn't like the other guys she's dated and that she isn't just another notch in his belt. He wanted her in every way possible and he planned on doing whatever it takes to win her heart. He picked up his phone and began dialing her number again. Still no answer.

"Where are you?" he said to himself. He ran his hands down his face, trying to erase the anxiousness that's taking forever to go away. He thought about calling her again but decided to text her instead.

Ron: Dinner later?

He waited and still no reply. He's never been the type to wait on anything. He was strong-minded and determined. Whatever he wanted he got and he wanted Lauren. His thought was interrupted by a knock at the door and he was glad. He needed something to take his mind off Lauren.

"It's open," he calls out.

The door opens to reveal Ron's best friend, Matthew O'Sullivan. "Hey, what's going on?" said Matthew as Ron stood up and greeted him with a bro hug.

"Yo, long time no see," said Ron.

"Hope I'm not intruding."

"No, not at all. Have a seat," he said as he took his seat behind his desk. "I haven't seen much of you since you tied the knot. How's the married life?"

"Married life is great actually. She keeps me busy. A busy that I enjoy a lot," said Matthew with a smile. "When the baby gets here I'm sure I will be even more busy, but it will be worth it."

"How is she doing? I haven't seen her car around lately?"

"She's great. Just doing a little too much, so the doctor put her on bed rest. So, I've been resting with her."

"Yeah," Ron laughed. "I bet you've been resting. If I had Lauren resting in bed, I don't think neither one of us would be resting."

"Speaking of Lauren, what's going on with the two of you? How was the date?"

Ron looked at his friend and wondered, what all did he know about the date, but it didn't take him long to piece together the bond between Lauren and her sister Layla. They were close and they probably talk daily.

"The date went ok. We went out, had dinner and a drink or two. Let me guess. Lauren told Layla about the date?" Ron asked.

"Yeah, but she didn't go into details.   She just said you two had a great date. I actually didn't think you would take my advice and ask her out again."

"Well, my first impression a while back wasn't my best. I told her I wasn't looking to settle down no time soon, along with other stuff. So yeah, I took your advice because I needed it. You know I'm not the type to beg anyone for their time, especially a woman," Ron stated.

"Yeah I know," Matt said with a grin on his face.

"What's funny?"

"Um, nothing. I'm just surprised you asked her out. You never listen to me," Matthew said as he threw his hands up. "Finally, my words are sinking in. Maybe you two will be tying the knot next."

"You're getting ahead of yourself. She needs to answer the phone first. I tried calling her several times today and no answer," he said as he looked at his phone.

"Just give her a minute, she'll call. She has a demanding job. She's probably just busy with work."

"Or maybe she's enjoying making me wait, or playing hard to get," Ron said as he got up from his desk and poured himself a shot of scotch from his mini bar. "Can I get you a drink?"

"No thanks, I should get going. I'm taking Layla out tonight. She's been cooped up in the house, so I decided to get her out for a little while."

"You're a good man Matt. I'm glad that things worked out for you. Hopefully, I will have the same luck."

"You will just give it time. Call me crazy but didn't you say before that you would never fall in love?" Matthew asked as he walked towards the door.

Ron laughed, "Why are you bringing up old stuff. I was young then, you can't hold that against me."

"Dude that was a few months ago."

"Whatever dude," said Ron.

"Well, I'm gone," said Matthew as he turned and left.

"Alright, be safe," Ron replied as he started walking back to his desk but stopped when he heard Matthew call his name.

"Hey, do me a favor and try not to break Lauren's heart. Her and Layla are close sisters and any hurt that she goes through, Layla goes through it. Right now, I don't need her going through a lot of stress," said Matthew.

"Don't worry, I'm not going to hurt her. You have my word," Ron replied.

Matthew said nothing but smiled at his friend before leaving out for good. Ron returned to his chair and began working. He needed to continue working to keep his mind off Lauren. He didn't want to fill her voicemail up like some crazy person, desperate for love and attention. After all, he did say he would never fall in love, but there was just something about her that kept reeling him in. He wanted to know more about her, but he can already tell it will take some time to do so. Just as he had given up for the day, his phone rang. He looked at it. It was Lauren, maybe she wasn't playing hard to get after all.

"Hello?" he answered.

"Hi, Ron. I'm sorry for returning your call so late," Lauren replied.

"No, it's ok. I was just busy with work. How's your day going?"

"It's going ok. Just anxious to finish up this case. How's your day going?" she asked.

"It's going the same as usual. Matthew stopped by not long ago. We did a little catching up. Seeing that it's been a while since him and Layla got married."

"Yeah, believe it or not, but it has been the same for me and Layla too."

"We've been kicked aside," he joked.

"Yeah, I totally agree. Ron, I just want to say, thank you for last night. It's been a while since I've been out. It was nice to get out and just have a nice time," she said with a smile. Just the sound of his voice had her blushing like a teenager in love.

"I guess I'm the one who should be thanking you. After being an asshole a few months ago, I didn't think you would even bother to give me another chance."

"Well, I guess I went against my better judgment," she laughed.

"Oh really? Was that after or before our lovemaking?" he asked.

"Hey, just so you know, I don't go around sleeping with hot guys."

"Oh so, I'm hot now?" Ron replied as they both laughed.

"A little."

"Just a little, ok I see. Well, I think you are beautiful and I'm lucky to have you as mine."

"So, you're staking claims now?" Lauren asked. She sat on the other end of the phone, twirling her hair between her fingers while blushing. She felt like she was back in high school and college. Butterflies all over again. Was she falling for him already?

"I am indeed. I think we should give whatever this is between us a try. Just so you know, last night isn't a one-time thing."

Lauren was glad to hear that last night wasn't going to be a one-time thing. She didn't know where his mind was after last night, but she's happy to know that they were somewhat on the same page. After dealing with Dewayne on and off, she didn't know if she could face trying to start another relationship so soon.

"We'll see," said Lauren. "Also, I won't be able to do dinner later. I'm staying late tonight."

"Ok, maybe another time?"

"Yeah definitely……I should get back to work. I just wanted to return your phone calls."

"Are you sure that's all?" he asked.

She wanted to end her day by packing up her work and racing over to his office, where he can throw her on his desk and make love to her all over again. "Yeah and of course to see how your day is going."

"Ok, well I should let you go so we both can get some work done. I will talk to you later."

"Ok, bye," said Lauren as they both ended the call.

Ron had a great feeling about them when he hung up the phone. He was smiling like a kid in a candy store. A first for him. This thing that he was feeling was the best feeling in the world. Is this what Matthew was experiencing? If so, he didn't want to ever let that feeling go. He looked up to see his new business partner Mark standing in the doorway.

"Someone has you in deep thought," said Mark as he came in and poured himself a shot of whiskey.

"I guess you can say that. What can I do for you?" Ron said as he locked his hands behind his head. He watched him down the first shot of whiskey before pouring another one.

Mark turned around and looked+ at Ron before taking a seat. "My mom wants me to visit her next weekend," he said.

"Ok go visit her," Ron replied.

"I can't go visit her. Every time I go to visit, she's always trying to hook me up with someone. I'm not ready to settle down. I have a few more bar nights left in me."

"Well just tell her you're seeing someone."

"Nope, doesn't work. When I show up empty handed, ten minutes later some chick is knocking at the door. You know, I love my mom, but she has terrible taste in women. You would think by now she would know my type."

Ron couldn't help but to laugh. He was glad he didn't have that problem. Even though his mother wanted him to settle down and start a family, she never pressured him or his brothers. "I wish I could say I know what you are going through, but I don't."

"Dude you have to help me," Mark asked.

"How am I supposed to help you?" asked Ron. "Why don't you just ask one of the women you go out with?"

"You know I can't do that. There're not the type to bring home."

Ron looked at him strangely but didn't bother to ask the kind of women he hung out with. "Well, I don't know what to say to you."

"What about the chick that came to visit you the other day? She definitely fits the bill," said Mark.

"I'm sure she does and she's off limits." The thought of another man touching Lauren in any way boiled his blood. He knew how Mark was with women. He's worse than he was.

"Ok, well does she have a friend or a sister?" Mark asked.

"Look, her sister is married, and I don't know if she has any friends."

"Ok, well is the sister happily married? Dude, I only need her for the weekend and maybe later," said Mark as he smiled.

"She's happily married and she's pregnant."

"Dude I can't take a pregnant woman with me. My mom will flip out and try to marry us on the spot."

"You couldn't take her anyway because she's married! For the record, she happens to be married to my best friend," Ron pointed out.

"Ok, your point is? Anyway, me and the guys are going out to this bar down the street later to catch the game and have a few drinks. You should come. You never know, maybe you will find you a hottie to take home."

"No thank you. I'm not interested," Ron said as he checked his email on the computer.

"You're not interested in finding a hottie or going out? Because both of them sounds good."

"Fine. I'll go out, but I'm not looking for a hottie."

"Ok cool," Mark said as he got up. "If you think of someone let me know.   Be sure to ask your girl if she has any friends."

"Yeah will do. I'll be sure to keep that in mind the next time I talk to her."

Finally, he had his office to himself again. Mark was right. He needed to get out and rest his mind. If things work out with him and Lauren, nights out with the boys would be rare, not to mention having a child. Nights out would probably not exist.

"Damn," he said to himself. What was he thinking? He was beginning to sound like Matt. A family, he didn't even know if Lauren wanted children or if so, how many? He was getting ahead of himself. Yeah definitely, he needed to get out.

CHAPTER SEVEN

Three hours later Lauren went against her rule of contacting the other party in her case, but it was the only way she could speed things up. She sat outside in her car with her briefcase in her lap, going through the paperwork she needed signed. She really didn't want to see Dewayne's face, but she had no choice. She didn't want to send Sunny to meet with him. She needed to stay far away from him as possible. Plus, she didn't know if Evelyn was still staying in the same residence as he. She took a deep breath and exited her car. She made her way up to the tall two-story white brick house with black shutters. The landscape was beautiful, which certainly had a woman's touch. She rang the doorbell and waited. No one answered, so she rung it again. This time she could hear footsteps. They were coming to the door. She was nervous. This wasn't a casual visit. She prepared herself as the door opened.

"May I help you?" said Dewayne as he stared at Lauren.

"Yeah…um, Dewayne, I'm sorry to intrude. I

tried calling, but you didn't answer your phone."

"Look, lady, I don't know who you are and why you are here anyway?"

"What?" She stared back at Dewayne after his last comment. Just like a man, always want to play dumb after shit gets out in the open. She didn't have time for his games. "Look, Dewayne, I don't have time for games and,"

"Neither do I. Now who in the hell are you and how do you know my name?" he said frustratedly.

Was he serious right now? Lauren didn't know what to believe. Was he pretending on purpose to not know who she was because he was ashamed that she found out that he was married or what? She didn't know, but right now she had a job to do and if he wanted to play dumb, she could play dumb too.

"I'm Lauren Hamilton since it seems like you have amnesia. I'm your wife's lawyer. You know, the wife you forgot to mention while we were trying to get to know each other. I'm representing her in her divorce case. She wanted a speedy case and the only way that can happen is if both parties consent to a mutual agreement." She reached into her briefcase and pulled out the documents that she needed signed and handed them to Dewayne.

He quickly snatched them from her and glanced over them. He seemed shocked that his wife was divorcing him. "You know, I don't know what you women are up to, but I don't have the time for games."

"What do you mean you women?" she asked.

"Someone came by yesterday causing a scene. Claiming I tried to play her. I had to threaten to call the police to get her off my property. I have no idea what she is talking about, just like I don't know what you are talking about now. You show up with some bogus divorce papers. I don't know what scheme you two are trying to play, but you will hear from my lawyer."

She tried her best to stay in a professional lane, but somehow that other side of her came out. "I can assure you, we are not the ones playing games here. If you would have been honest in the beginning, neither one of us would here at fucking your door. Because you got caught up in your lies, now you want to act all innocent and act like you have fucking amnesia. Just sign the fucking papers and mail them to me or drop them off at the address on the envelope." She said what she had to say then turned and left. She could feel his eyes on her as she hurried to her car and got in. "Fucking Sunny," she said out loud before driving off.

She drove in silence until she reached her office. This was supposed to be her lunch break, but instead, she spent it confronting a fake ass absent-mindedness asshole. She grabbed her things out of her car and made her way inside. The main person she needed to see was at her desk.

"Sunny," she said as she tapped on the counter. "I need to see you in my office please."

"Ok, give me about ten minutes…."

"Now Sunny, its urgent!" she called out.

"Dang ok, here I come," Sunny said as she slipped her shoes on and followed Lauren to her office.

"Close the door behind you," said Lauren. She was upset, and it showed.

"Are you ok? You seem irritated."

Lauren took a seat at her desk and looked up at Sunny. "Did you go visit Dewayne yesterday?"

"Oh, about that…"

"Sunny! Why would you do that? You are part of the case. What if she was there?"

"But she wasn't," Sunny replied.

"You don't know that. Don't go there again. Not until this case is over," she said, but quickly changed what she had just said. "As a matter of fact, don't even bother going there after the case is over. He's no good and he's not worth going to jail over."

"Ok so, what about you?" Sunny asked.

"What about me?"

"What were you doing there?"

"Dale wants me to speed up the process. The only way to do that is to get Dewayne to agree that it's what they both want. When I got there, he got all amnesia on me. Like he didn't know who I was."

"Yeah tell me about it. He was the same way when I made a surprise visit yesterday too. I just wanted to confront him and let him know what a jerk he was. You know what? He threatened to call the cops on me."

"Yeah, he mentioned that. He also mentioned that we will hear from his lawyer and I do not want to hear Dale's mouth when he finds out what happened. I could lose my job."

"I'm sorry. I will say that it's my fault," Sunny said sympathetically.

"No, it will be ok. I just need to try to focus and fix this, but right now I could use a stiff drink."

"You know what? There's a nice bar nearby. You want to go?" Sunny asked.

"When I said stiff drink, I was thinking more of chilling at home."

"You always chill at home. The day is almost over with. Let's just go have a few drinks, talk chill and leave?

Lauren thought about what Sunny was saying, but her mind was also on the case. She didn't need to be out having drinks. She needed to spend every second and every minute on the case.

"I don't know Sunny. I really need to focus on the case. All my energy needs to be on the case. If not, Dale is going to chew my ass off."

"You work too much. Getting out will only help

you focus. Sometimes we think better after we give our brain a rest."

"You're right," Lauren replied.

"I am?" Sunny was shocked that Lauren agreed with her.

"Yeah, you're right. Maybe I need to take a break and clear my thoughts."

"Ok well, I am going to finish my work for today and so don't leave without. Plus, I didn't drive today." Sunny left out of the room before Lauren could change her mind about going out.

A few hours later, Lauren finished up the remaining of her work and checked emails. She grabbed her purse and headed to the women's room to freshen up. She stared at herself in the mirror. She was working herself too much on this case. She needed a nice bath and sleep. After spending several minutes freshening up, she made her way up front where Sunny was waiting for her.

"Any longer in there, I was going to come and get you," said Sunny.

"I was just freshening up. I didn't want to frighten anyone," Lauren replied.

"You looked fine, now lets' get going before Dale has you staying late."

"Good idea."

They both hurried out the door and got in the car. Sunny checked her makeup once inside as Lauren drove.

"So where are we going? Lauren asked.

"Andy's Bar and Grill. It's just a few minutes away. I go here a lot for lunch. They have awesome food. Nothing major, but it's filling."

"I've never been there. Even though I've passed it a few times. I hope the food is as good as you say it is because I am starving."

"You are always starving. You need to eat."

"What? I do eat."

"A cereal bar is not considered a meal. It's not considered real food!" said Sunny as she placed her nude lipstick on, followed by her gloss.

"Everyone is not lucky like you. You get to eat a house and still not gain weight. So yeah, I try to watch what I eat."

"Well tonight, you're going to eat."

Ten minutes later they pulled up at Andy's Bar and Grill. Both ladies double checked themselves in the mirror. Fixing their hair again and applying makeup.

"Alright, let's go. I'm so hungry I could eat just about anything right about now." They made their way inside and began scanning the place for somewhere to sit.

"You want to sit at the bar?" Sunny asked.

"No, I rather sit somewhere I don't have to worry about falling on my ass," Lauren replied.

"What about over there?" Sunny asked as she pointed to an empty booth located near the corner. "It's even facing the tv."

"Yeah, that's even better. Let's hurry before someone takes it."

After taking their seats, they were greeted by a waitress that handed them a menu. The menu was short. Lauren quickly decided and handed the menu back to the waitress. They both settled on a large pizza and salad. She didn't bother to have a stiff drink since she was driving, so she went with a sparkling water instead.

"I thought you said they had a lot of food here?" Lauren asked.

"Nope, I never said they had a lot of food. I only said they had great food. Meaning the food that they have is great," said Sunny with a smile.

"Next time I am picking the place."

"No way. You would have us chilling in a coffee shop. Who wants to chill in a coffee shop?"

"There's nothing wrong with a coffee shop. You can basically do the same thing you do here?

"Like what? Read a book in silence, while I sip on a mocha latte? No way I don't think so," laughed Sunny.

The waitress returned with their food and they immediately began eating. The food was really good. Either that or the fact that she was starving. She felt bad for not having dinner with Ron. She wanted to call him back, but her pride stopped her. Just the thought of getting too close scared her, even though it's what she wanted.

"You know we should confront that bald-headed liar," Sunny stated.

"Who are you talking about?" Lauren asked.

"Dewayne of course. I still can not get over the fact that he was going to call the cops on me. Like really. Was it that crucial?"

"We were on his property, he had the right to do so. We, especially you, shouldn't have gone to his house. Lets' just hope nothing bad comes out of our visit." Lauren was trying to make partner at the firm. She didn't need or want anything to stop her from doing so.

"Lets' go shoot some pool," Sunny suggested as she stood up and grabbed her drink. Rule number one was to never leave your drink unattended.

"I don't know how to shoot pool."

"Don't worry I can show you. Now get your drink and follow me.

Lauren grabbed her drink and followed Sunny to the pool area. "You know, you are worse than my sister. You two would make great friends and I bet……" Her voice slowly drifted away as she spotted a familiar face shooting pool. Surrounded by a bunch of thirsty hoes, she couldn't tell he was enjoying their fake laughs or not.

"Girl, who are you staring so hard at?" Sunny asked. She looked straight ahead, and it didn't take Sunny long to figure out who Lauren was staring at. "Dang girl he is fine. You know him?"

"Yep that he is and I know him. I know him really well," said Lauren as she continued to stare at Ron.

"Oh, so that's your man surrounded by hoes?"

"He's not my man. Let's just go back to our table. I'm not in the mood to be confrontational right now." Lauren turned to walk off, but Sunny grabbed her by the wrist.

"I know this isn't you walking away. This is not you girl. The girl I know wouldn't walk away from anything she loves."

"I don't love him."

"Well, you could have fooled me. No one stares at a man like that if she didn't love him or feel some type of way about him."

Lauren stared into blank space. She was right, who was she fooling. Maybe love was a pretty strong word, but she did feel some type of way about Ron. Seeing those girls all in his face just made her think he was still playing the field. She really didn't know what to think, but there was only one way to find out.

"I just want you to know that you are bad a influence," said Lauren.

"Yeah, so I've been told."

"How do I look?" she asked.

"You look great. Stop procrastinating and get over there and get your man," Sunny replied.

"He's not my man!" Lauren said through her teeth.

"If you say so," said Sunny as she stood there beside Lauren who continued to stare from across the room . "Look either you walk over there, or I will make an announcement."

She didn't know if Sunny was joking or not, but she wouldn't put anything past her. "Ok, fine I'm going. Just don't do anything crazy ok…I got this."

"Ok, your man awaits."

"Sunny."

"I know, I know he's not your man."

Lauren quickly reapplied her lip gloss and gave her hair a toss. "Ok, here goes nothing." She turned and walked shyly as she made her way through the crowded space. Everyone seemed to be enjoying themselves as they cheered and drank their beers. She could still see him. He was laughing at whatever the blonde whispered in his ear. The shortest distance between them seemed like a million miles away. She was just a few steps away. She hoped that he would notice her first by feeling her presence, and he did.

CHAPTER EIGHT

Ron looked up and saw the one person that has been on his mind all night. At that moment, no one in that room existed but her. No one was as gorgeous and beautiful as Lauren standing before him. He wasted no time leaving the company that stood around him. He made his way to Lauren, then pulled her into his arms and gave her a kiss that let everyone in the room know that she was his and he was hers. He only stopped to come up for air as he placed both hands on the side of her face and whispered softly against her lips.

"Hi," he said.

"Hi," she replied with a shy smile. "I promise I wasn't stalking you."

"You can stalk me any day love. What are you doing here? I didn't take you for a bar type girl."

"I'm here with a co-worker. She suggested coming here after a very long day for both of us, but I swear I had no idea that you were going to be here."

"I'm actually glad to see you. You're the best thing that happened tonight. After losing three games in eight ball, I was beginning to feel terrible. Then you show up and now I'm better."

"Wow, so you're just as bad as me?" she teased.

"Considering I already won four games, I would say I did pretty good. It was just hard to focus when my mind was on someone else," he said as he looked Lauren directly into her eyes.

He was good. He was really...good. "Looks like your friend over there isn't liking the idea of you talking to me," Lauren said as she nodded her head in the direction of the blonde that kept staring at them.

"She's not my friend. I don't even know her name and I don't care to know it. I was thinking about leaving soon. I didn't want to come, but a good ole co-worker talked me into it."

"Really? Because the same thing happened to me. She's around here somewhere," she said as he looked around. "Actually, she's right over there," she pointed, "with some strange guy standing too close to her."

Ron looked up in the direction Lauren was looking at and laughed. "He's not a stranger. That's Mark. He works with me and he is also the guy that talked me into coming out with the guys for a drink. He's harmless. I promise."

Lauren could see the two laughing and having fun. She always felt Sunny was more like a sister, so she felt the need to be more protective over her. She knew what her sister went through with previous boyfriends and didn't want her or anyone else going through the same thing. She felt the urgh to go over there, just to make sure he wasn't a weirdo preying on innocent women, but she took Ron's word. Plus, Sunny was grown. She tended to make good decisions and hopefully, this was one of them.

"Have you eaten yet?" Ron asked.

"Yeah, just a few slices of pizza. It wasn't the best, but it sure does beat a cereal bar any day."

"Tell me about it. I had the hot wings and they were ok. I think it was because I was hungry."

"I felt the same way. A steak would have been better," she replied.

"If you are free sometime, I would love to take you out to dinner again to get that steak?"

She couldn't believe what she was feeling right now. The butterflies returned, and she was blushing up a storm. She knew it was noticeable, but she didn't care. There was something about him that made her not want to worry about anything that was going on in her life. He made her feel like at that moment, nothing and no one else mattered. It was just the two of them.

"I would love that," she replied.

"We can shoot some pool if you're up to it?"

"Um yeah sure, but I have to say that I do not know how to play," she stated as they walked towards an empty pool table.

"You've never played pool before?" he asked.

"Only on my phone, and yes I know it's not the same."

"Tonight, is your lucky night, I'm in the mood to teach," said Ron. He grabbed a pool stick and placed it in Lauren's hand. He then stood behind her as he directed her every move.

As she leans over, she could feel his hands on her waist. His closeness made her feel some type of way. The smell of his cologne had her senses going insane, while his touch had her completely unable to focus on what she was doing. She drew the pool stick back as she tried to aim but missed when she felt his hardness against her ass.

"Oh goodness," she said out loud and the balls on the table went everywhere but in the hole. "See, told you I wasn't good at it."

"Just try again. How about I stand back and give you space, so you can focus?" he asked.

Space wasn't what she needed right now. She needed something else and it wasn't space. Her mind vaguely flashed back to their recent lovemaking. He was a nice length and thick. Yeah, it wasn't space. She smiled to herself, "Um sure, but I'm telling you space or no space, I'm just not good at it," she said as she went for another shot and still nothing. On her third shot, she finally got two balls in. She turned and looked at her with joy in her eyes and went up to hug him.

"You're a natural," said Ron. "Soon you will be beating me."

"I doubt that, but then again you did say you lost a couple of games tonight," she said as she let his hands pull her close.

"Hey, I only lost a few games because my mind was occupied on you."

"Is that right?"

"How about I show you just how much I missed you." He said nothing else.

He then let his body do the talking instead as he lowered his head and devoured her lips. With every second, he grew harder and harder. His manhood was straining against his zipper, bulging out so far. He pulled her as closely as he could so that she could feel just how bad he wanted her. When the kiss ended he looked her directly in the eyes. She didn't have to say a word, he could tell she was feeling that same way he was feeling. Horny as hell.

"I, um…I need to go to the restroom," she said.

He slowly released her from his hold. "Don't take long," he said as he gave her another kiss before letting her go.

Lauren walked as fast as she could towards the restroom. She didn't stop until she was inside. She checked the two stalls and they were empty. She hated using public restrooms, but this was an emergency. She needed some air and she needed it quick. Another minute with him would have caused her to lose all carefulness. She was sure she would end up with soaked panties before the night was over and she was right. She went over to the sink, took a paper towel and dampen it with water before applying it to her face and neck. Now that her upper part was cooling off, she needed to do something about the lower part.

"Just calm down girl, get it together," she said to herself as she closed her eyes for a moment of quietude, but that soon ended as she heard the bathroom door open. She wasn't cooled down all the way, but this would have to do. She threw away her paper towel as she rounded the corner and ran into something solid.

Lauren stood there in a daze. She wasn't thinking straight, and she didn't care. She threw her arms around his neck as they began kissing uncontrollably.

"You know it took every ounce of me to not throw you over that pool table and make love to you, so that everyone would know for sure you are mine," said Ron as he lifted her up and wrapped her legs around him, causing her skirt to raise up above her thigh.

"Staking claims again I see," she replied.

"You know who you belong to. It's only just a matter of time for you to see it." He placed her back against the wall as he pressed into her so that she could feel just how hard she was making him.

"It wouldn't work out with us. I'm too focused on my career and trying to build a name for myself," she said between kisses. "Plus, I've been told I'm too headstrong."

"I admire you for wanting to make a name for yourself. Just remember, you're never too headstrong for me, you just need someone who can tame you," he whispered against her lips before kissing her again.

She didn't know what to say, so she said nothing at all. She let her body do the talking and right now it was screaming for him as she felt his hand slide her panties aside and began playing with her. She let out a pleasure filled moan.

"You're so ready for me," said Ron.

Before she knew what was happening, all she could feel was the head of his cock rubbing against her clit before making an entrance. He was hard and seemed bigger than the last time they were together, but it felt so good and so raw. He was fucking her raw. She should stop him, but he was already in and it felt so good. He pumped harder and harder as he kissed her neck before returning to her lips. He reached down and touched her clit again while he continued to make love to her. Since she was already wet from the start, it was only a matter of time before she explodes. His rhythm increased. She knew he was getting closer.

His breathing increased. He should pull out, but

he wanted to show her who she belonged to. She was his and it was time that she knew that. He gripped her ass tighter as his speed increased. He grunted in her ear as she held on tight, they were both getting close. Then together came their powerful release. He pulled out and spilled his seed in the seat of her panties before plunging back in.

"Next time there won't be any pulling out," he whispered against her lips as the sweat trickled down his face.

Lauren didn't say a word. She was still trying to catch her breath too. After a few minutes, she was finally able to say something. "I think we should probably pull ourselves together before someone comes in."

"Yeah, you're right," he replied as he slowly pulled out of her.

They quickly got them themselves together. Lauren stayed behind as Ron left out first.

"What the hell just happened?" she thought to herself. "Two nights in a row, this can't happen again."

CHAPTER NINE

The next day Lauren walked into work with a smile on her face. Despite the ongoing case, she still felt like she could conquer the world right now. She wasted no time in getting into her office and began working immediately. She didn't see Sunny up front. She was probably running late. They both had a long night and for Lauren, it was the best night ever. Just the thought of last night had her smiling from ear to ear. She still couldn't believe what had happened last night. She told herself that she wouldn't give in to Ron's sweet talk, but somehow, she didn't listen. The end resulted in hot sex in the women's bathroom.

"Hey, Lauren girl!" said Sunny as she peeped her head in Lauren's office.

"Welcome, I'm glad you decided to come to work today."

"I got you something." She handed Lauren a mocha latte. "I had to drop my sister off at work, so I decided to grab you something to drink."

"You have a sister?" Lauren asked as she took a sip of her well-needed drink.

"Yes, and she can be a pain in the ass sometimes, but I love her dearly."

"You never mentioned before that you had a sister. I always thought you were the only one."

"Yeah, well I have a brother too. So, I guess I am somewhat the only one. We didn't grow up together. They are from my dad's side. I just recently found out about them." Sunny took a seat in her main sitting place, in front of Lauren's desk and slowly sipped her drink.

"Oh wow, I know that must have taken you by surprise."

"It did, but what doesn't kill you, makes you stronger right? Plus, they are my family and family are everything. I also get the chance to play big sister."

"I'm sure you are the best big sister."

"Oh, I almost forgot, Evelyn called before we left yesterday and said she will stop by this morning," said Sunny.

"What? Sunny why didn't you tell me this bef9*+ore we left yesterday?"

"I didn't want you to not enjoy yourself. You needed to get out and get your head off the case for a second. If I would have told you, you would have ended up staying even longer. Which, by the way, would have caused you to miss your little episode with your man."

"How many times do I have to tell you, he is not my man or boyfriend, We are just close friends."

"Yeah," said Sunny as she slid to the edge of her chair and leaned over and whispered. "Look, I don't know who you are fooling. That man is yours. You two disappeared for a while and let's not forget your twisted skirt afterward."

"He is not my man and I'm getting tired of repeating myself." She tried to ignore Sunny by checking her voicemails. Ron wasn't her man. There was no use in pretending that he was. As soon as she agrees to date Ron, he will probably be just like the other men. Right now, maybe she will just enjoy his company.

"Have you seen the way he was looking at you? He may not be your man, but you are definitely his woman," said Sunny as she crossed her legs and snapped her fingers. "I saw the way he was all over you."

"Ok, enough about me. What about you and what's his name?"

Now it was Sunny who pretended to not hear Lauren as she sipped her coffee. "I have no idea what you are talking about."

"Un huh, yeah you do. I saw the way he was all up on you."

"He wasn't all up on me. He was showing me how to play pool."

"What? I thought you knew how to play pool?" Lauren asked.

"I do, but he doesn't know that. Guys love to rescue a damsel in distress," she said as she smiled. "Anyway, his name is Mark and he seems nice."

"They all do at first," Lauren replied.

"Exactly, that's why I didn't call him. He gave me his number, but I refuse to call. You should have seen the way he was staring the women up and down. Clearly, he's not finished playing the field and I will not be another link in his chain."

"Well, if you do decide to call him,0 please be careful. Speaking of being careful, when Evelyn comes, try not to be up front. I don't know if she will recognize you or not."

"If she didn't recognize me before, I doubt if she will recognize me again."

"We don't know that. I just don't want any problems. She is a scorned woman and you know sometimes a scorned woman is nothing to play with. Plus, you have come to be a good friend and worker. I don't want anything to happen to you."

"You mean that?" Sunny said with a smile.

Lauren was sincere about it. Sunny had become a good friend. She had proven that she can be trusted. That and the fact that she sees so much of Layla in her. "Yes, I mean it from the bottom of my heart."

Sunny jumped up from her seat and hurried around to Lauren's side of the desk. She then bent down and wrapped her arms around her neck, hugging her as tight as she could. "I always wanted a big sister."

"Please let go of my neck," Lauren said through her teeth.

"Oh sorry. I can get carried away sometimes. Anyway, I need to get back to work before Dale sees me. I swear he acts like he can never do anything for himself. Make copies, call the courts, schedule appointments, call the clients and make coffee."

"Sunny I hate to be the one to inform you, but that's included in your job duties. Well, everything except for making coffee."

"You know what, I quit."

"What?"

"I quit making coffee."

"Oh, for a second I thought you were…...never mind, but I do thank you for the coffee. You really shouldn't have. It can get expensive buying coffee every day you know."

"Don't worry about it. My sister started a job up the street a few weeks ago at this coffee shop and let me be the first to say, the coffee is the bomb.com and I don't have to pay. How cool it that?"

Lauren was about to say something until she saw

Dale walk past the door. She knew he was probably looking for Sunny. The only time he comes out of his office is when he couldn't reach Sunny on her desk phone and when he was expecting company.

"I think Dale is looking for you. He just walked past the door and knowing him, he'll be calling your name any minute now."

"Ugh! oh well, guess I will see you later." Right as Sunny was about to leave, they could hear Dale's voice calling for her. "Told you and I bet he doesn't want anything but coffee." She turned around and within a few steps, she ran into Dale.

Lauren could hear the two talking, but she had other things to do, rather than to listen to Sunny get lectured about coffee. If he didn't bother her about the case, she was good. Everything was moving along, but it wasn't fast enough for them. Cases like this took time. Why couldn't Evelyn understand that and why did Dale pretend to not understand. This wasn't his first rodeo.

"Good morning Lauren," said Dale.

Lauren looked up to see Dale standing in the doorway. "Good morning Dale."

"How's the case going?" he asked.

"Oh, it's going as expected. You know these types of cases take time."

"I see." For a minute he stood there and said nothing. Which made her nervous.

Apparently Sunny wasn't the only one getting a lecture today. "Look, Dale I'm sorry about yesterday. I…"

Dale held up his hand cutting her off. She didn't know what he was going to say, but she wished that he would just get it out for Christ sake. She just wanted to get her lecture over with, so she could carry on with her day.

"I spoke with Evelyn today. She informed me that she hasn't had any updates about the case. She's wondering, what are the court dates?"

"It's only been two days Dale," said Lauren.

"I gave you this case because I knew you would work your magic and speed things up."

"I can't work that kind of magic and you know it. I tried to pull some strings, but nothing. I've sent emails out asking for a speedy case, but no good. They all needed reasonable cause to expedite the case. I'm doing my best to find that cause, so I can speed things up."

"This is your first solo divorce case. It can make you or break you," he stated.

"Yeah, I know."

"I'm counting on you. Try not to let me down," he said before leaving out.

She was glad to see him leave. She's only had the case for a couple of days and he's expecting her to make a miracle happen. Was there something he wasn't telling her? Now she just had one more person to deal with whenever she arrives, and that person was Evelyn. Until then, she needed to call every source that she had and search everywhere that she could for answers.

She spent part of her morning researching and responding to Ron's texts. She thought about telling Ron about her recent encounter with Dewayne but decided to wait. She began texting him to ask for a favor, but it was just too much to ask in a text. So, she decided to call him instead and he picked up on the first ring.

"Hello gorgeous," said Ron.

"Hi, I hope I'm not bothering you or called at the wrong time."

"Never. I'm just going over some paperwork. How's your day going?"

"It's going ok. Just looking into some stuff with my case and I sort of need a favor."

"Ok, how can I help you?"

Lauren thought of several ways to tell him that she went to see Dewayne but couldn't think of the perfect way to say it. So, she just said it.

"I went to see Dewayne yesterday," she said nervously.

"I don't think I like the way this is heading. You want to see him again?"

"What? God no," she laughed.

"Good," said Ron.

Lauren could hear him exhaling over the phone. He was certainly the jealous type. Another reason why they wouldn't make a good couple. She didn't have time for the jealous type. She didn't need someone following her or watching her every move because they felt insecure.

"Don't worry, it was work related."

"Wait a minute, if he's Evelyn's husband, what are you doing contacting him without his lawyer?"

"That's the part I'm getting too. My boss has been riding my ass since he's given me this case. He wants me to rush things. I'm trying, but I'm getting nowhere."

"And the only way to do that is to get both parties to consent to a mutual agreement," said Ron.

"Exactly, but when I went there, he was acting strange. He acted like he didn't know who I was."

"Maybe he was just embarrassed that you found out that he was married."

"No…I don't think that was it. Sunny made a surprise visit the day before and she said he was the same way with her. That's why I need you to do an extensive background check on him."

"A background check?"

"Yeah. I've done all that I could do, and I've come up empty handed each time. Someone is hiding something. I can feel it Ron. I understand just wanting to get everything over with for the sake of moving on with your life, but I'm telling you…." Lauren got quiet as she heard Sunny's voice up front.

"Hello?" said Ron, but there was no answer from Lauren. "Hello? Are you there?"

"Ron, I need to call you back," she whispered.

"What's going on?" he said with concern in his voice.

She could now hear her boss's voice trying to defuse the situation. Lauren quickly ended her call and made her way up front where all the commotion was happening. She sees Sunny and Evelyn exchanging words with Dale standing between them.

"What's going on?" said Lauren as Dale turned around and looked at her.

"Seriously, what's going on?" Evelyn repeated. "My husband has blocked all my accounts thanks to you and your sidekick visit."

"Oh, I'm so sorry. I was just trying to speed things up," said Lauren.

"Speed things up. How? By making him take away everything from me!" Evelyn yelled.

"Look, why don't we go into my office and we can discuss everything?" Lauren asked.

Evelyn didn't bother to speak to Lauren or Sunny. She stood there ignoring them as if they didn't exist and spoke directly to her boss Dale.

"I'm going home, and I expect for this to be taken care of immediately. If I don't get my money back, you won't get paid and you know what that means," Evelyn said in a low tone to Dale. She looked up at Lauren and Sunny with a look to kill before storming out of the door.

"Sunny you are fired," said Dale.

"What!" said Lauren and Sunny in unison.

"You heard me, and Lauren I need to see you in your office," he said before walking away.

"Let me talk to him," she whispered to Sunny. She then hurried to her office where Dale was leaning against her desk.

"Close the door behind you," he said angerly.

"Look, I can explain."

"Please do because right now I am upset and disappointed in you. You know you are not allowed to contact the other party.

"You wanted me to speed things up. You and her both. You two have been riding my ass about this case. I'm doing my best Dale to speed up this case with very little information that I have."

"This is your best? I've seen you do better than

causing a ruckus between two parties."

'I just need more time, I swear I can fix this."

"Well, your wish is granted. If the case is contested it will take more time than we have. I don't care what you do, but you better fix this as soon as possible," said Dale as he turned to leave.

"What did Evelyn mean about what she said before she left?"

Dale stopped and turned to Lauren. He was in no talking mood right now and it showed. "It means what it means."

"Oh, and Dale one more thing. I really need Sunny on this case. She's been a great help. If you want me to speed things up. She has to stay."

"She really has been a great help. Look at where she's gotten you."

"C'mon Dale. If I find someone else, it will set me back and I don't have time to go over this case with someone new. She's already informed and know what needs to be done."

"Fine, I'll think about it," he said before leaving out.

Lauren stood there with her mind in deep thoughts until it was interrupted by her cell phone. She already knew who it was, her sister. She hadn't spoken to her last night or today.

"Hello?" said Lauren.

"Hey, are you ok?" Ron replied. "You gave me a scare."

"Oh, hey. Yeah, I'm ok."

"What happened earlier? You sounded like something was wrong."

"Just a little confrontation out front. Evelyn showed up and let's say things got a little ugly. She was super upset. Are you calling to give me some findings on Dewayne?"

"No, it's too soon to find out, but I will keep you posted on whatever I find. I was just calling to make sure you were ok."

"How sweet of you, but thanks, I am good." The thought of Ron being concerned about her well being made her smile. Maybe he was a good guy after all, but only time will tell.

CHAPTER TEN

Lauren packed her things up into her briefcase. It was getting late. After six to be exact. Today was a quiet day for her. Dale hasn't been to work the last two days. He said he was sick and didn't want anyone else getting sick. He decided to work from home instead. He was still bothersome but not as much. So, she took this time to catch up on other cases that she has been neglecting. She hadn't talked to Ron all day as well. Just a few texts from him with one stating that he needed to talk to her soon and that he will explain everything later.

"Hey," Sunny said as she peeped her head inside of Laurens office door.

"Hey, I thought you left already?" said Lauren.

"No, well I was going to, but I didn't want to leave you here by yourself. Seeing that it is Friday the thirteen," she said with an eerie grin.

"Really? I know you well enough to know that's not the reason. Plus, I don't believe in that Friday the thirteen stuff." She began shutting down her computer and switching up her shoes from the flats to her heels.

"Well, do you believe you can give me a ride home?"

"See, I knew it was something else. You can not fool me. How many times do I have to tell you, if you need a ride just ask? I don't mind taking you home or picking you up for work. It's the least I can do for being so helpful on this case."

"Maybe a raise?"

"Don't push it. Although, I did talk to Dale about giving you a pay increase."

"Oh really! What did he say?"

"As much as I expected him to say. It wasn't in the budget right now."

"That's Dale. Cheap, cheap and cheap. He probably uses that plastic cling wrap stuff for condoms," said Sunny as they both laughed.

"Where do you get this stuff from?" Laughed Lauren.

"What? It's true. The next time you are in his office, check out the bottom drawer. Nasty I tell you. Just nasty."

"I'm not going anywhere near that man's office," said Lauren, "Ok I'm ready."

Lauren closed her door and locked it. Everyone

was already gone for today. She looked up at the clock and noticed it was twenty minutes to seven. She was glad Sunny decided to wait on her. This was the latest she has ever stayed at work.

"I have to go to the restroom. I've been detoxing from sodas and invested in drinking more water."

"Yeah, go ahead. I will wait here for you."

"Thanks, I'll make it quick," said Sunny as she hurried off.

Lauren rested her feet by having a seat in one of the chairs. She looked at her phone and saw missed calls from Ron and her sister. She began texting her sister first. It was late and she didn't know if she was asleep or not. Seeing that the text was from three hours ago, while Ron's text was a little over an hour ago. She knew her sister was probably asleep.

Lauren: Hey just leaving work. Dropping Sunny off 1st then I'm heading home. Love Ya!

Layla: Yes, I'm still up. Call me, please!! Not feeling good.

Lauren: Ok. I will swing by instead. Give me about 25 mins.

Layla: Thanks Sis.

Just as Lauren began dialing her sister's phone number, she could hear her phone in her office ringing. The office was closed for the day. No one should be calling at this hour, so she ignored it until it stopped ringing. Within a few seconds, it started ringing again. This time she decided to answer it. She got up from her chair and reached over on Sunny's desk to answer her phone.

"Watson & Associate Lauren Hamilton speaking." The line was silent. "Hello, can I help you?" she asked but there was no answer. She was about to hang up the phone until she heard someone breathing on the other end. "Hello?" she called out again and still no answer. "Hello?" The called ended.

"Who was that calling at this time of the night?"

Lauren placed the phone back on the receiver. "I don't know. They didn't say anything, but I could hear someone breathing."

"Ugh, breathing like having sex breathing or sleep breathing?"

"Neither. Just a regular breathing."

"Maybe their ass called you?

"What? You mean pocket calling?"

"Ass calling, pocket calling it's all the same. Now lets go I'm starving."

"You're always starving," said Lauren.

"Look who's talking. I didn't eat much for lunch and I didn't eat breakfast. You know breakfast is the most important meal of the day."

"Yeah, yeah, so they say."

Lauren and Sunny made their way to the front door where they noticed a yellow envelope. They both looked at each other.

"I didn't hear anyone knock earlier," said Sunny as she opened the door and grabbed it. "It's addressed to you," she said as she held it out to Lauren.

Lauren took the package from Sunny. She was curious to find out what was inside and wasted no time in opening it. The look on her face caused Sunny to look at what was in Lauren's hand.

"What is it?" Sunny asked as her eyes roamed the photos Lauren held in her hands. "Wow! Isn't that your man?"

Lauren didn't say anything as she scrolled through the photos before placing them back in the envelope. "We should get going. You mind if we swing by my sister's? She's not feeling well, and her husband is out of town."

"Sure."

Lauren and Sunny were both quiet on the way to Layla's house. A million things were going on in her mind all at once. Just when things were going good between her and Ron this shows up. Just when she thought she could let down her wall, he goes and messes things up.

"You want to talk about it?" said Sunny.

"No. there's nothing to talk about. He's not my man. He's free to see anyone he chooses to see." Lauren followed the circular driveway and parked her car in front of her sister's house.

"Wow, your sister's house is nice. You want me to stay in the car?"

"No, of course not. You can finally meet my sister. You two have so much in common. I promise I won't stay long. We're both tired and I'm sure you have plenty to do on your weekend."

"No, not at all. My sister and I were supposed to go shopping, but she's working. So, I might just sleep in."

They stood outside of Layla's house as they rang the doorbell. She should have used her spare key, but she figured her sister was up. She stood there with her mind still on the photos of Ron. Ron having dinner with some woman. Photos showing him laughing and then hugging on her.

"You know, it could be someone framing him. Don't worry yourself over it."

Lauren looked at Sunny and didn't say a word. She knew what Sunny was thinking. She seemed as if she wanted to say something else but didn't. Every time Lauren worried about something, she carried that expression on her face. She needed to get it together so that her sister wouldn't see her worrying too. Just as she was about to press the doorbell again, the door opened.

"Hey sis!!" said Layla as she greeted her sister with a hug before looking over at Sunny.

"Hi, I'm Sunny," she said as she extended her hand.

"I didn't know you were bringing company," said Layla as she shook Sunny's hand.

"It was quickest to just come right over," said Lauren.

"I don't mind," said Sunny. "I've heard so much about you."

"Hopefully good," she smiled. "Oh, please come in. I will go get a third glass."

"A third glass for what?" asked Lauren.

"I got us a bottle of fake wine. I know how you like to have a glass of wine and you know I can't drink right now. So, I got the next best thing," she called out from the kitchen.

Seconds later, Layla walked into the living room where Sunny and Lauren were sitting carrying a glass and a bottle of Welch's Sparkling Rose. She placed the glass down on the coffee table and began to open the bottle. She then filled each glass.

"I thought you were not feeling good?" asked Lauren.

"I was, but I'm feeling better now. Trapped gas,"

she said as she filled each glass.

"Oh… ok well, I wish you would have said something. We could have been home by now you know."

"Yeah, I know, but I haven't seen you in forever. It's been a while since we chilled. You've been so caught up at work, I just don't get to see you as much."

"Layla, its only been a few weeks."

"Seems like forever to me. So, how's things going with you and Ron?"

Both Lauren and Sunny looked at each other after that comment was made and took a sip from their drink. Layla noticed the look both gave, especially her sister. She knew her sister too well to know when something was up. She could just forget about it, but that wasn't her.

"I wish this was the real thing," Lauren whispered as she downed the drink in her glass.

"What was that look for?" Layla asked.

"What look?" Lauren replied.

"That look that you do when you don't want to talk about something."

"So, spill the beans. What's going on with you two?"

"There's nothing going on with us. We're just friends."

"Just friends? What are you not telling me?"

Lauren said nothing as she looked at Sunny, giving her the don't say a word look. Sunny wouldn't dare say a word, or would she?

Layla turned and looked at Sunny, right as Sunny turned her head away from both and remained silent. "Sunny do you care to share?" asked Layla.

"I'm not saying a word. You two are not going to get me caught up in you all's shenanigans," said Sunny as she held her empty glass. "And where is the real shit?"

"You tell me the details and I will tell you where the real shit

is," Layla said as she smiled.

"Is that all that you have?" said Lauren.

"Someone sent photos of Ron with another woman to our job today!" yelled Sunny.

"What!" Layla and Lauren said in unison.

"Sunny! How can you tell my business like that?" said Lauren.

"Sorry, but she blackmailed me," said Sunny.

"She was testing you!"

"Well, it worked," she said as she got up from her seat and held up her glass. "Ok, now where's the real shit?"

"In the kitchen in the wine fridge," Layla replied then turned her attention back on her sister. "How long ago did this happen?"

Lauren took a deep breath before responding. "Tonight. Someone left this at the door as we were leaving out tonight." She reached into her purse and pulled out a large envelope containing the photos and handed them to her sister.

"Lauren, maybe he was framed."

"That's exactly what I said," said Sunny as she came walking in with a bottle of wine. She stopped to fill up Lauren's glass before having a seat.

"Have you talked to him today?" Layla asked.

"No, and I don't plan on it."

"Look, Lauren I really think you should call him and hear him out," Layla suggested.

"He was only hugging her. That doesn't mean anything. So what, they were having dinner. That doesn't mean anything either," said Sunny.

"She right," Layla agreed. "It could be his sister or his mom."

"Really? Better yet, it could be his wife. Just like lying ass Dewayne," Lauren stated.

"Damn, she's right," Sunny said to Layla. "She's got a point. It could be the wife or baby mama."

"Sunny you are supposed to be on my side. Anyway, what I'm trying to say is to not make a big deal of this before finding out more information. Who sent this and why? Apparently, they have a motive to break the two of you up."

"You can't break up something that never was together," Lauren replied.

"That definitely was not the case the other night," said Sunny.

"Wait what? What happen?" Layla questioned.

"Nothing happened," Lauren said as she looked at Sunny. "It's getting late and we really need to get going. I'm glad you are feeling better."

"It was nice meeting you," said Sunny. "We all need to do this again." She took one last gulp from her glass before walking to the door where Lauren stood.

Layla followed behind and reassured her sister that everything would be ok before giving them both a hug.

"Thanks sis. I'll text you when I make it home."

"Or call, I'm sure I will be up. It's hard to sleep without Matthew."

Lauren only nodded ok as she smiled. She was glad her sister was happy and in love. She could only hope that one day she will be as happy as Layla.

They drove in silence on the way back to their side of town. Mainly because Sunny was asleep from a little too much to drink and the combination of them staying late at work. She was tired too. Thank God it was Friday. She would have ended up working from home if it wasn't.

"Sunny wake up," said Lauren as she pulled into the driveway of Sunny's house.

Sunny slowly opened her eyes and sat up from her slumped over position. "I'm so sorry I fell asleep. I must have been really tired."

"It's cool. It has been a long day for the both of us. Thank God it's the weekend."

"I know. Well, thanks again for the ride," Sunny said as she exited the car. "Enjoy your weekend and Lauren, no work. You work too hard," she said before she turned and walked away.

Lauren waited inside of her car until Sunny was inside of her home before driving off. She then arrived at her apartment ten minutes after dropping Sunny off at home and waited in the car before getting out. She was tired and exhausted. She looked around her neighborhood. It was quiet and dark outside as she reached into backseat and grabbed her purse before getting out of her car.

She unlocked her door, walked in and tossed her things aside in a chair before turning on the lights. "What the fuck are you doing in my place!" she yells.

CHAPTER ELEVEN

Lauren stood there staring at Dewayne as he sat on her sofa. "I said, what are you doing in my place?" She was furious, and it showed.

"Calm down, I just want to talk," he stated.

"Oh, so you know me now? Just the other day you acted like you didn't even know who I was and now you show up uninvited in my place."

"I miss you."

"Go to hell," she said as she reached for her purse, but was too late. He snatched it away right as she reached for it. "Give me my purse!"

"Sit down and let's talk. We have so much to talk about." He patted the seat of the sofa next to him. "Have a seat," he demanded.

Lauren could hear her phone ringing in her purse. It was probably Layla. If only she could answer it. Then the ringing stopped. Just as she was about to give up hope, it began ringing again.

"I need to answer it."

"You think I'm crazy? What? I let you answer it and then you run call the cops? I don't think so, sweetie."

"I'm not your sweetie," said Lauren as she stepped backwards. She didn't want to be near Dewayne or have anything to do with him. She watched him make his way off the sofa and walk slowly towards her. For every step he took, she took a step backward towards the kitchen counter. She could still hear her phone ringing.

"I really need to get that. It's probably my sister or boyfriend. If I don't answer it, they will be kicking this door in to make sure I am ok."

He looked at her as if she was joking and like he was some kind of fool. "Where is the paperwork?"

"What are you talking about?"

"The paperwork for the case! Where the fuck is it!" he yelled.

"It's at the office!"

"Stop lying. Don't fucking lie to me!" he yelled again before taking the back of his hand and slapped her across her face.

Lauren grabbed her face. She could tolerate a lot of things, but a woman hitter wasn't one of them.

"Payback is a motherfucker," she said as she quickly reached for the half-empty wine bottle. With all her strength she threw her arm back and smashed him across the right side of his face causing him to wince in pain.

"You fucking bitch!" he screamed as he held his bloody face.

She took advantage of the moment and tried to escape, but he grabbed her by the arm and pulled her back. She had to think quick and she did. She slid out of her blazer and made her way to the door right as it opened. Her heart sank when she saw the front door open, but then suddenly it began beating with joy at the sight of Ron. At that moment she didn't care about the photos from earlier. She was just relieved to see help.

"Ron!" she called out to him.

With anger on his face, he wasted no time in marching straight towards Dewayne to show him what happens when someone attacks his woman. He was so quick that Dewayne didn't see the fist that smashed into his face. He fell back and then charged forward towards Ron but was met with another punch and then fell to the floor. He was out.

Ron looked over at Lauren who stood there holding her phone against her ear. Her eyes showed fear as she exhaled. She was scared. More like terrified.

"Are you ok?" Ron asked.

"Yeah," she replied as she took a deep breath.

"Thank you." Her voice was shaky as he walked over to her and held her close. "The cops are on their way. I thought…."

"Shhh it's ok," he whispered before capturing her face in his hands. "Did he hurt you? Because if he did, I swear I will make him pay for…."

"He didn't hurt me," she said cutting him off. What she really wanted to say was "No, but you did." But right now, just wasn't the time. "He only slapped me, but I'm ok. I promise. I did fight back as you can see." She pointed to the broken wine glass and fragments on the floor.

"Good." It was the only thing he said as he held her tighter, but eventually let go when she pulled away.

She wanted to stay in his arms forever, but the sight of him holding another woman crossed her mind. Holding her the way he was holding her right now. She walked away just as a knock came to the door. They knew it was the cops from the blue lights echoing through the window, but Ron wanted to make sure whomever came through that door went through him first.

"Good evening officers," he said as he let them in. "He's right over there." He pointed to the floor where Dewayne laid. "Don't worry, he's alive, but he won't be if he puts his hands on my woman again."

The officers arrested Dewayne and threw him in the backseat of the squad car. Lauren and Ron stood outside her apartment talking to the other officers that had pulled up on the scene and gave them a police report. She just wanted this night to be over with. She looked up at the squad car and noticed Dewayne staring at her and smiling, but that smile faded when Ron looked over at him. They each had madness in their eyes and someone wanted revenge.

They finished up their statement with the officers and made their way back in. Tonight, was definitely a very long night and all she wanted right now was to clean up the mess and take a hot shower. As much as she wanted to be alone right now, she knew she would sleep better with Ron there. She felt safer around him.

She grabbed the broom from the closet and began cleaning up the mess that was made. "I could have really used that wine right about now," she said as she continued cleaning up. Now that everything was over, she had questions and wanted answers. "How did you know to come here?"

"Matt text me asking me to come check on you. He said your sister was getting upset because you were supposed to call, and she hadn't heard from you."

"That sounds like Layla."

"He didn't want her to get upset, so he asked me to stop by to make sure you were ok and I'm glad I did." He walked over to her and removed the broom from her hands and pulled her close for a kiss. The moment he kissed her he could feel the tension from her body dissipate.

His embrace and sympathy weren't what she wanted, it was what she needed. She could see how worried and sincere he was, and her heart begin to melt. She wanted to fall in love with him, but again her heart wasn't for sure. Not after seeing those photos. Maybe they were staged, but how could they be staged when you could clearly see his face and hers?

"Who is she?"

"Who is who?"

"Don't lie to me Ron. Who is the woman you were having lunch with and hugging?" she asked again while trying to maintain her cool.

"Sweetie I don't know what you are talking about?" he replied.

Lauren pulled away. She was about ready to throw his ass out for acting like he didn't know what she was talking about. She reached into her purse, pulls out the photos and thrust them to him. She watched him as he carefully examined them.

"Who gave you these?" he asked.

"It doesn't matter cause from the way you are acting right now, these photos must be real and she's someone you apparently care for."

"Of course I care about her," he replied as he scanned through the photos.

Lauren stood there with her heart breaking into

pieces. Those words hurt more than anything in the world right now as she stared at the floor. She couldn't bring herself to look at him.

"Lauren, I care for her because she's my sister."

"Your sister?" she asked.

"Yeah. I was meeting with her because she's not in a healthy relationship right now. She needed a place to stay where her husband wouldn't find her. I have a safe house. I had someone to escort her there. I wanted to make sure she wasn't followed and…."

"And the pictures prove that someone was following her," said Lauren. "Oh God, I feel so stupid."

"Remember when I texted you earlier letting you know that I needed to talk to you about something?"

"Yeah."

"That was it. She's going through a divorce. I know you have a lot on your plate now, but I had wanted to see if you would take her case?"

"Oh God, I really do feel so stupid right now. You must think I'm this crazy woman."

"Stop saying that and no, I don't think you are crazy. I would have thought the same thing. You didn't know about her."

"So, you're not mad at me?" she said as she wrapped her arms around him.

"No, I'm not mad," he said with a smile as he leaned in and devoured her lips in his. "I could never be mad at you," he said between kisses.

"You promise?" she said as she looked up into his eyes.

"How about I show you."

"I think I would like that," she replied. Even though she had a long night and was tired, she could never get tired of what he was about to give her.

She took him by the hand as she led him down the hallway to her bedroom where they partially undressed. They couldn't keep their hands off each other as they made their way to the bathroom where they finished undressing the lower half of their bodies. Ron turned on the shower and stepped in and reached out for Lauren to take his hand. He pulled her in the shower where he placed her back against the wall. They began kissing as his hands roamed all over her body. The sounds that escaped Laurens lips made him harder and harder.

He bent down in front of her and placed both hands on her legs. "Hold on," he said as he lifted her legs over his shoulder.

Lauren prepared herself for what was about to come. Seconds later she felt his tongue devouring her. Sucking and licking and sucking, Rotating his tongue around her clit. She was sure the neighbors heard her, but she didn't care. Her moans became louder as her body danced against his tongue. His tongue had her feeling like she was floating high and she couldn't hold on any longer.

"Ron," she said as she moaned his name. She couldn't hold on much longer.

He knew he was bringing her to the edge of desire and couldn't wait to join her. He eased her legs down and kissed his way up. Stopping at her breast and taking her nipples in his mouth before taking her lips.

She braced herself when she felt the tip of him at her entrance. She spread her legs wider, letting him know she was ready to take all of him. He stared her in her eyes as he drove into her. Filling her up with every inch of him as he moved in and out of her. She wrapped her arms around his neck as his arms held her tightly around her waist. With each stroke and thrust he was claiming her as his. His pace became faster and faster until he couldn't take it any longer. He was coming and he was going to come fast. He needed to pull out, but she had her legs wrapped out him so tight, he didn't bother to resist. He gave in and spilled his seed, coating her inside.

She could feel him as his hot seed spilled inside her and overflowed her as it seeped out and began running down her legs. Thank goodness they were in the shower and thank goodness she was on the pill.

CHAPTER TWELVE

The next morning Lauren laid in Ron's arms thinking about last night. First their hot shower scene and then last night's run in with Dewayne. Something didn't seem right or was she reading into things like she usually does.

"Good morning beautiful," said Ron.

"Good morning to you," she replied with a smile as he kissed her forehead.

"Did you get any sleep?" he asked.

"Of course. Thanks to you. I just want to say thank you again for yesterday," she stated as she sat up in bed.

"Baby, I told you, you don't have to thank me. I'll do it all over again if I need to. I'm just glad I got here before things go even more out of control."

"Thanks."

"Speaking of this fool. How did he get in?"

"You know, I don't know. I checked the windows and all I can think of is…he came through the front door."

"He has a key?" Ron questioned.

Lauren could tell by the tone of his voice that the thought of Dewayne having a key irritated him. "No, I never gave him a key," she quickly responded.

"You need to get your locks changed."

"Yeah, I know."

"I'm serious Lauren. This isn't something you should put off."

"I know Ron. I will get it taken care of."

"When?" he asked as he looked up at her with his arms behind his head.

Lauren rested her head back against the headboard and closed her eyes. He was right, but she didn't want to think about it. At least not right now.

"Today. I will get it taken care of today," she said as she stared down at him. He was so handsome. She couldn't get mad at him, even if she wanted to.

"Great, now give me a kiss," he said as he reached up for Lauren. He was gentle as he pulled her in for a simple kiss before staring into her eyes.

"What?" she whispered.

"You're beautiful," he stated right as his phone began to ring. "I'm not going to look at my phone. It's the weekend and I want to spend it with you."

"You gotta answer it. You never know, it could be your sister or work," she stated to make sure he wasn't lying about having a sister.

"You're right," he replied as he reached over and retrieved his phone off the nightstand. "It's Mark." He looked at Lauren as if he preferred not to answer the call.

"Go ahead, answer it. I'm going to shower," she said before heading to the bathroom. She could still feel the existence of last night's love session. She wanted to take this time to shower alone. As she prepared herself for her shower, she listened in on Ron's phone call.

"Yo, Mark what's up? No, I'm just over at a friend's house."

"A friend's house?" she repeated to herself. "A fucking friend." She was in such deep thought that she didn't hear Ron at the door calling her name.

"Lauren…Lauren?"

"Yeah."

"I need to run to the office for a few minutes. Maybe we can catch up later?" he asked.

Lauren opened the bathroom door with her robe wrapped around her. The sound of the shower was drowning out the sound of Ron's voice. She remained calm as she opened the door to hear what he had to say.

"I couldn't hear you over the running water," she said calmly. She didn't want Ron to know that she was upset.

"Mark called and said he needed to see me at the office. I was hoping we could get together later?"

"Um, yeah sure. I did tell Sunny I would hang out with her today and help with some things," she lied. Deep down inside Lauren knew she didn't want to see him later, but every time she sees his brown eyes, it was hard to say no.

"Good. I'm really sorry about this."

"It's fine," she said in a dry tone of voice.

"You sure? I can call him up and reschedule."

"No, it's cool. Trust me I am ok. I had plans anyway remember?"

"Ok. Well, I'm just going to get dressed and I will shower at work." He leaned in to give Lauren a kiss on the lips but caught her cheek instead. "What's wrong?"

"Nothing. I just haven't brushed my teeth yet. You know..... morning breath."

He only smiled. "Women," he said out loud. "Don't forget to change your locks."

"Yeah…I won't." He gave her one last kiss on her forehead before getting dressed and then leaving out.

She didn't bother to walk him to the door. She waited until she heard the door closed before exhaling the anger she was holding in.

"Fucking friend! I can't believe this shit!" she said before jumping in the shower. She needed to get her day started and find something to do to get her mind unwrapped from around her so called friend Ron.

Lauren pulled up at Sunny's house. She didn't bother to check her makeup or hair like she normally does. She marched her way to the front door and rang the doorbell. She was upset. Not about last night, but about overhearing Ron telling Mark that he was over at a friend's house. Just when she thought they could be more, he had to ruin it.

Sunny opened the door to a pissed off woman. This wasn't the same Lauren she worked with the last couple of years. This was a different side that she had never seen before.

"Hey girl come in. What's going on? You sounded upset over the phone."

"You are not going to believe what happened," said Lauren as she walked in and had a seat on the sofa. Her eyes wandered around Sunny's house. It was her first time in her house. "You have a nice place here."

"Thanks, it belongs to my grandmother, but that's not what we are discussing right now. Let's talk about the reason why you are here. You never visit me!" said Sunny as she flopped down on the same sofa with Lauren. "Fill me in, what's going on? It's man problems, isn't it?"

"First of all, yes. Secondly, he's not my man."

"Lauren girl, you are in denial. That man wants you."

"Yeah maybe so, but as friends."

"What? What are you talking about? Have you seen...."

"He called me a friend!" Lauren yelled. "A friend Sunny! A fucking friend!" She was damn near in tears.

"Ok, wait a minute. Am I missing something? Didn't you just say he wasn't your man?"

"Yes, but still. We've been having awesome sex and going on amazing dates. After last night's lovemaking, I figured we were more than that."

"Wait. So, you two did the do? I knew it. I knew it. That day when you came in with a little pep in your step. I knew something went down," Sunny said as she gave a little smile. "Carry on."

"I'm having a crisis here. Where's the wine? Please tell me you have wine?" Lauren asked.

"Of course. How do you think I make it through the work week dealing with Dale?"

Sunny excused herself as she went to the kitchen and later returned with a bottle of wine and two glasses. She poured herself and Lauren a good amount for the first round. Before she could set the bottle down, Lauren's glass was just about empty.

"Are you serious?" Sunny asked.

"Serious about what?" Lauren replied.

"Your glass is almost empty. You have like two drops left. Has anyone ever told you that you might be an alcoholic?" Sunny joked.

"I'm not an alcoholic, but yeah my sister may have mentioned it before. Anyway, can we get back to the real issue here," she said as she poured herself more wine.

"You know what the issue is here? You love him."

"What? Are you crazy? You are supposed to be taking my side here. I don't love him."

"Do you smile for no reason when you think of

him?" Sunny asked.

"Yes, but that doesn't mean anything."

"Do you get butterflies whenever you are around him?"

"Yes! But that still doesn't mean anything. Are we forgetting the real issue here? He called me a friend."

"What do you want to be called?" Sunny asked.

"I don't know. Just not a friend." Lauren pouted.

"Look, I don't know why he called you a friend. All I can say is follow your heart. You need to be honest with him about how you really feel."

"I can't do that. I just can't."

"And why not? If a man looked at me the way he was looking at you, I guarantee you he would be mine and vice versa. I can't even get a man to buy me a drink."

"What about his friend Mark? Seemed like you two were hitting it off good."

"We were, along with every other woman in there. I need a man that will have eyes for me and only me. I like that man of yours."

Lauren gave Sunny that "he's not my man look" but Sunny wasn't falling for it. No matter how many times

Lauren said he wasn't her man, she wasn't falling for it. That night at the bar, he made sure everyone in the room knew who she belonged to.

"No matter what you say, he is your man. I think you are just afraid to get your heart broken again."

"How do you know I've had my heart broken?"

"What woman hasn't. Hell, I've had my heart broken a few times. You would think I would learn from the first one," Sunny said as she shook her head. "I kept falling and eventually I got tired of being hurt. I know there is someone out there for me. I'm not giving up on love and you shouldn't either. That man loves you."

Lauren rolled her eyes at that last comment. "He doesn't love me. If he loved me, he would say it and he wouldn't called me a friend."

"Sometimes love is often shown rather than said. Would you rather for him to say it or show it?"

"I…I don't know. Both." she replied with uncertainty. "Why am I sitting here venting to my assistant?"

"Because I am a good listener and the best assistant."

"Yes, you are, and I want to say thank you for listening to me vent and actually giving me some good advice. I usually call my sister, but I didn't want to upset her."

"Well, I am glad you finally trust me enough to vent to me. I'm one of the good ones. I won't tell your personal business around the office. I know how you feel about that."

"Thanks," Lauren said as she sipped the last of the wine from her glass.

"Refill?" Sunny asked.

"No, no thanks," said Lauren as her phone began to ring.

"I wonder who that could be?" said Sunny with a grin on her face.

Lauren looked at her phone then back at Sunny. "It's him. My so-called friend."

"Ok, well answer it."

"If I answer every time he calls or text, it will make me seem needy or desperate."

"That's not true. Just answer the damn phone!" Sunny yelled.

"No!"

"You're killing me here," said Sunny. "How about

140

we go get something to eat instead?"

"Now that I can do," Lauren replied.

"Ok great! Do I need to change or anything?"

"No, you look fine. Just put on some shoes. I know a nice place where we can go that is casual."

Lauren's phone began to ring again, and she ignored it. She wasn't about to fall in love for anyone that only sees her as a friend. Starting today she was taking advice from her rule book. Never make yourself available all the time for a man. Give him a chance to miss you and that's what she was going to do.

CHAPTER THIRTEEN

Lauren and Sunny took a seat in a booth at her favorite restaurant The Pier. The service was busy as usually, but they were able to get their order in. For a minute Lauren stared into open space. Her mind was still on the friend comment that Ron made earlier. Why would he make love to her and then call her a friend? Before she took things further with him she needed to know where they stood with each other.

"Hey, snap out of it," said Sunny as she snapped her fingers. "How are you going to invite me to lunch and daydream of someone else?"

"Well, technically you invited me."

"Yeah whatever. You know if your friend has a friend, be sure to give them my number."

"I thought you weren't looking for love?"

"I never said that. I'm open to dates and maybe more."

"Honestly, I don't really know anyone. I've never met any of his friends, not even Mark."

"Maybe we all can do a double date?" said Sunny.

"Um, I don't think so," Lauren said as she laughed.

"Why? I think it would be nice. We can do dinner and karaoke."

"Who does double dates nowadays?" Lauren asked.

"Come on, it'll be fun. You need to let your hair down for a change."

"Ok, I will think about it. As soon as I get something to eat," Lauren replied as she pointed to the waitress walking towards them with their food. Her phone began ringing. It was Ron. She quickly hit the ignore button. A few minutes later she received a text from him stating that he needed to talk to her and that it was urgent.

"Is that Mr. Lover Boy calling you?" Sunny joked.

"Yep, it's him."

"Why don't you just answer it? He could be calling

to apologize. You just never know."

"I doubt it. Do men ever apologize?" Lauren asked as she waited for an answer, but Sunny was too busy eating. "You're eating like you haven't eaten in days."

"I didn't eat much yesterday and this morning I didn't eat breakfast."

Lauren and Sunny ate their food and discussed the case for a bit. She even mentioned to Sunny about what happened after dropping her off. That night she saw a different side of Dewayne that she never thought she would see.

"I can't believe that shit," said Sunny. You know what I don't understand? How come he remembered you then?"

"That's a good question. He definitely knew who I was, that's for sure."

"Why didn't he remember who we were when we paid him a visit? I think he's playing some sick joke on us," Sunny stated.

"We need to just keep our distance from him. Especially since now we know what he is capable of doing."

"Have you thought about getting a restraining order or against him?"

"No, I haven't. I don't think I need to. After last night I don't think he will be get getting out any time soon. Maybe things will cool down and he will be his old lying self again," Lauren said as the waiter brought them their bill.

"I don't know. After last night, I think you should look at getting a restraining order. It's better to be safe then sorry. That's what you always say at work."

"It's not the same."

"I know it's not the same. It's even worse because it involves your life," Sunny said as she wiped her mouth before taking a sip of her drink.

"Look at you, being all cautious," said Lauren.

"I know. I believe you are rubbing off on me."

"Ok, there's nothing wrong with that. That's a good thing."

"Oh no it's not. You are a workaholic with no life outside of work," said Sunny, causing Lauren to gasp.

"Sunny!"

"What? It's true," she laughed.

"I do too have a life outside of work. It may not be as wild as yours, but I do have one," Lauren stated as

Sunny stared at her with a smile on her face.

Everyone in the office knows that Lauren probably didn't have a life outside of work. She was a hard worker that tends to take her work home with her. No matter how hard she tried to separate her personal life from her job, she always ends up choosing work. Maybe Sunny was right. The more she thought about it, the more she realized that she does work too hard.

"What's on your mind?" Sunny asked.

"Nothing…………ok I was thinking about how you may be right. I do work too hard. I take work home. I do it so much until it feels normal, but you know what?"

"No, but I'm dying to know," said Sunny.

"When this case is over, I am going to take me a long vacation."

"Are you serious? You have never taken a vacation. At least not since I've been working there. I have to see it to believe it."

"Well, just watch me. Are you ready to leave?"

Sunny took the last sip of her drink. "I'm ready now."

They both placed their cash down on the table before exiting their seat. They then made their way out of the restaurant where the sun was beaming down. Lauren grabbed her sunglasses from her purse and placed them on her face.

"It feels so nice outside today," said Sunny. "I do have to say that the food was really good, but it was cold as hell in there. I had to cover up my nips so they wouldn't fall off."

"It wasn't that cold." Lauren laughed. "Next time bring a jacket," Lauren said as she searched for her keys in her purse as they continued to walk to the car.

"Oh my gosh!" Sunny said as she looked over her shoulder. "Whatever you do don't freak out."

"What are you talking about?" she asked as she turned around and saw what Sunny was referring to. "What the hell?" Coming towards them, she saw someone familiar walking her way.

"I thought you said he was in jail?" Sunny asked.

"He is or was," she said confusedly. "Let's just get out of here."

They picked up their pace. The faster they walked, the faster Dewayne was walking towards them. His pace increased as he tried his best to catch up with them. This was one time she wished she had on her flats.

"Oh my goodness he's getting closer. Hurry up and unlock the door!" Sunny yelled.

"I'm trying. I can't find my keys!" Lauren replied hysterically as she dug through her purse.

"Hurry up!"

"Oh God! Ok I got them!" she screamed with joy as they both got in the car.

"Lock the door! Lock the fucking door!" yelled Sunny. Lauren quickly locked all the doors just as Dewayne made his way to the car and began yelling.

"Hey! I need to talk to you," he said as he knocked on Lauren's window. "Hey! I'm fucking talking to you!"

"After what happened last night, I don't have anything to say to you! Stay away from me!"

Dewayne looked at Lauren as if he didn't know what she was talking about, but kept demanding to talk to her and that it was urgent.

"He's crazy and delusional. Let's just go."

Lauren put her foot on the pedal and placed her car in reverse. She wasn't listening to anything Dewayne had to say as she backed her car up and drove off. She could hear her phone ringing in her purse. She knew it was either her sister or Ron, but right now just wasn't the time.

"Are you ok?" Sunny asked. She could she see

how worried Lauren was.

"Yeah, I'm ok," she said as she drove.

"I hate to sound so cliché, but I think you might need to get a restraining order," Sunny stated.

Lauren didn't say a word. She looked over at Sunny who was looking as serious as ever. "I hate to admit it, but I think you might be right. You feel like taking a ride with me to the police station?"

"You know I have your back. Do what you have to do," Sunny replied.

The day just got interesting. There was something about Dewayne that just didn't seem right. Something about him seemed different.

CHAPTER FOURTEEN

The next day Lauren woke up to a knock on her door, followed by the sound of her phone ringing. She checked her alarm clock on the nightstand.

"Oh gosh," she said through her groggy voice. "It's after ten. I must have been super tired."

The knock on her door subsided. She reached for her phone, then tossed it aside after seeing five missed phone calls from Ron. She laid back on the bed and closed her eyes. She didn't want to talk to him right now. She did miss waking up next to him and how he always did her body right. The sex was out of this world. It was the best she's ever had. Just thinking about it was making her body crave for him. She closed her eyes as she touched her breast. She then traced her hands slowly from her breast, down to her stomach. She imagined it was him touching her. Her sheets still smelled of him, which was making her moment even more enjoyable. Even the sound of his voice made everything seem real. Like he was there in her place. The sound of Ron's voice made her quickly open her eyes. Was Ron inside her place?

"Lauren!" he called out from the living room. "Lauren!"

"Ron?" she replied as she quickly grabbed her black robe to cover her nude body. "Ron is that you?" She made her way out of her room to see him standing in the kitchen, leaning on the counter. "Ron, what are you doing here? Better yet how did you get in here?"

He wasted no time in cutting straight to the point. He never was the type to bite his tongue about anything to anyone. Not even to the beautiful Lauren who was standing there in her short black robe. "Where were you yesterday? I've been calling you nonstop," he said as he stood there staring at her. The sight of her standing there was beginning to wake up parts of him that would cause him to forget the reason why he came there.

"I was out with Sunny. We had a girl's day out," she said as she began to make a pot of coffee.

The faint smell of her perfume as she passed him gave him a semi erection. He was trying to control himself. "You were that busy that you couldn't pick up the phone for a second to see what was wrong?"

"Something was wrong?" she replied as she looked at him.

"No, nothing was wrong. I just wanted to give you the information that you requested that I look up for you."

151

"Oh, that's right. I almost forgot about it. So, what did you find?" she asked.

"Don't, do that."

"Do what? I'm just asking if you found anything."

"What happened yesterday at The Pier?" he asked bluntly.

"Nothing happened," she said as she tried to avoid his gaze. "Coffee?"

"No thanks. I just want to know what happened at The Pier yesterday."

"And I told you nothing happened. Sunny and I had lunch and talked about the case."

"So, you're telling me Dewayne didn't chase you two after leaving out of the restaurant?"

"Who told you that?" she demanded as she waited for his response.

"So, it's true?"

"I didn't say it was true." She took a sip of her coffee and wondered how did he find out?

"You didn't say it was false either."

"Are you following me or have someone following me?"

"No to them both."

"Ok then, well how did you find out?"

"Don't worry about how I found out. When stuff like that happens, you need to call me."

"I took care of it," she stated.

"Yeah I know. You filed a police report and a restraining order."

"Who told you?" she demanded.

"A buddy of mine. He's a detective."

"Gosh. What happened to privacy?"

"When it comes to you, I want to know if something is wrong. I rather hear it from you then from someone else and if someone is trying to hurt you, they will have me to deal with me," he said as he stared directly at her while looking into her eyes. He wanted her to see that he was serious and meant every word that he said.

She turned away with her back now facing him. Saying those last words were making her feel some type of way. She wanted to throw herself at him so that he could have her for breakfast, but she needed to stay cool and calm. She couldn't give in to him so quickly. "I can take care of myself."

"I know you can, but that's not what I'm saying," he said as he stared at her from behind. He could see the fullness of her ass. He wanted to walk right over there where she stood and show her exactly what he was talking about.

She could feel his eyes on her, undressing her to the full extent and making her moist down below. She wondered if he was hard and feenin for her the way she was for him. "I don't need you to take care of me FRIEND," she reiterated as she turned around.

"I see where this is going," he said with a slight smile on his face. He knew exactly what she was referring to. "You're upset."

"I'm not upset."

"Yeah you are. You're upset about me calling you a friend," he stated.

"Nope." She opened her dishwasher and began loading yesterdays dishes it in. She was trying not to bend too far over, since she was naked underneath her robe. "I'm not mad."

"I think you are mad. Now I know why you didn't answer your phone." He watched her bending over as she filled the dishwasher up. Bending over was how he wanted her. On all fours, slurping every drip of her from behind. She knew what she was doing, and it was working. He came over to discuss the findings on her case but found himself wanting something much more. He's had enough of looking. His manhood was throbbing and pushing against the zipper of his pants, just ready to be released. He walked over and stood behind her, causing her to slightly jump when she felt his presence.

"What are you doing?" she asked as she tried to turn around, but he had her pinned against the counter with her back facing him. As he pressed his body against her, she could feel something hard and solid pressing against her lower back.

"Do you really think I could make love to someone I call a friend?" he asked, but she remained quiet. The smell of his cologne was intoxicating, which was causing her not to think straight.

"I… I don't know. You tell me," she whispered.

His hands went around her waist, untying the belt that held her robe closed. She should stop him, but she was too weak. As soon as her robe came open, his hands went straight to both breasts. Be then began cupping them before tracing the tip of her nipples, causing them to harden under his touch. He wasn't near finished with her yet. He let one hand slip down between her legs. He rubbed one finger around on her clit, caressing it before slipping it inside.

Her body began moving against his hand right before he pulled it out. "If I was just your friend, do you think I would do this?" he stated as he then took his finger and began sucking off all her juices on it. "I don't think so," he said into her ear before turning her around and devouring her lips.

She wanted to push him away, but he had a hold of her and the way he was gripping her ass, she knew he wasn't planning on letting her go any time soon.

"I want you," he said against her lips.

"Show me," she replied.

He grabbed her by the hand and lead her to her bedroom where he removed her robe. "Get on all fours," he demanded, and she did as she was told. He got behind her pressing her back down, so that her goodness was exposed to him. He hurried out of his clothes and stoked his cock. He couldn't wait to bury himself in her, but first he had other intentions.

"Ron, what are you…oh my gosh!" she screamed right as she felt his lips on her from behind. She could feel his tongue going in and out of her, licking her up and down and sucking on her clit. If she was mad, she wasn't mad anymore. She was in pure ecstasy as her moans got louder and louder. She snatched her pillow to bury her face into it so that her moans wouldn't wake the neighbors. Just when she thought it was over, he plunged into her.

Every frustration that he had he took it out on her ass. With each thrust he branded his initials in her. He could feel her muscles gripping his cock each time he pulled out. With him still inside of her, he then coerced her to lay flat on her stomach as he continued fucking her from behind. He leaned over her and kissed the side of her neck.

She could tell when he was about to come. His rhythms began speeding up. The faster he went, the harder his thrust became. They both were breathing hard until finally they both exploded. She covered his thick rod as he filled her up until he was spilling out of her. Their breathing slowly subsided as he fell onto the bed, pulling her against him.

"I wonder how we ended up in bed?" she said jokingly.

"I don't know, but never wear that short robe around me. Especially bending over with nothing on under it. You just might find yourself in the same position."

"Is that right? Well, in that case I will try my best to keep that robe around," she said as they both laughed, but with all jokes aside, she still had some questions. "You know…you still haven't told me how you got in?"

"I picked the lock," he replied.

"What?" she said curiously as she repositioned herself facing him. "What do you mean you picked the lock?"

"I used a paperclip to jimmy the lock. The same lock you were supposed to get replaced."

"Well, you could have just asked for a key. Anyway, what was so important that you had to break in to tell me?"

"I think we should get dressed before we discuss this. I have something I want you to look at," he stated.

"This sounds interesting."

They showered together and minutes later they

both were seated on the living room sofa where Ron handed Lauren a stack of papers.

"What is this?" she asked.

"I looked into Dewayne like you asked and you're not going to believe this. The guy you and your co worker was dating isn't Dewayne."

"He isn't Dewayne?" she said as she stared at the papers in front of her.

"No. Not according to the information there. His real name is Derrick Vance."

"How could that be? I saw his driver's license. His name even showed up as Dewayne on my caller ID. Are you sure? I even looked him up and his picture matched everything."

"Derrick is Dewayne's twin brother."

"Oh my goodness. I guess that explains his incognito personality. Is there anything else?" she asked.

"Derrick is also a convicted felon."

"On what charges?"

"Murder," he replied.

"What!" She jumped up and began pacing the floor. Just the thought of her dating a murderer sent chills up and down her spine. "Are you kidding me right now? Because if so, this is a cruel joke you are playing on me."

"Baby I wouldn't dare do that to you. When I got the information, I tried calling you as soon as possible, but you wouldn't pick up the phone."

"I'm sorry. I'm so sorry. I was mad ok," she said as she sat down beside him.

"Mad about what?"

"Mad that you called me a friend."

He reached for her hands and held them in his. "Baby, you know I was only joking," he laughed.

"Do I? So, what do we do about this Dewayne or Derrick guy?"

"Stay away from him. I don't want him going anywhere near you. He's a dangerous person and if you see him…you need to call me. Just like you should have done yesterday."

"How long are you going to hold that over my head? I told you I'm sorry."

"And I accept your apology. Just don't let it happen again. I was worried about you. Did he touch you?"

"No, he didn't. We rushed to the car and locked the doors. After that I went and filed a restraining order."

"Good. That's a start. Hopefully he will stay away. I would hate to hurt him."

"You're not going to hurt anyone. You're not that

kind of evil person."

"I will if anyone put their hands on you or threatens you," he said as he kissed her hand.

Lauren didn't know how to feel. Her heart was beating with joy. Every moment she spent with him, she felt like he could be the one, but only time will tell.

"Ron, is Dewayne…I mean Derrick. Is he still in jail?"

"No, he was bailed out." He searched through the papers and found a mugshot of him. "Here," he said as he handed Lauren the mugshot.

"I don't think he was the one that followed us yesterday."

"How do you know that?"

"I hit Dewayne, Derrick in the face with the wine bottle. He had a cut about his right eye. Just like here in the photo," she said as she pointed to the photo. "When we saw him yesterday, he didn't have a scar." Her voice began to crack when she thought about the grave mistake that she made.

"What's wrong?"

"I got the restraining order on Dewayne…not Derrick. Gosh, what have I done."

"It's ok. We will go get everything cleared up. Ok?"

"Ok. Thanks."

"In the meantime, I think you should stay with me or with your sister. Anywhere but here."

"Ok. What about Sunny? You have to promise me that she will be ok too. We are both working on the case. She's my assistant Ron."

"I will make sure she's safe. I will have Mark watching her. He won't let anything happen to her. I promise he's good. He will protect her. Do you think you can work at home until this is over with?"

"Um, yeah. I will need to go in tomorrow and grabs some things."

"Ok, I will take you."

"No…I mean thanks, but I will be ok."

"Just check in so I will know you are safe. That's all I'm asking. Can you do that?"

"Yeah. Yes sir captain," she said as she kissed him on the lips.

"I love you," He said against her lips.

Those words meant so much to her. They were the missing link to what she wondered, but for some reason, she couldn't say them back.

CHAPTER FIFTEEN

The next day Lauren was a nervous wreck. She hurried into work with Ron trailing her in his vehicle. A few minutes later Sunny showed up with Mark following her. He stayed far behind, so she wouldn't be suspicious.

"Hey, I got you some coffee. What you doing here early?" Sunny stated. "You never beat me in to work."

"I'm only thirty minutes early Sunny and I think you are a little late."

"Who me? Never. Well, maybe a little. Anyway, I think someone was following me. Oh, and here is your coffee. Have you heard from Dewayne yet?" she rambled.

"Thank you Sunny. No, I haven't heard from him and thank God, but I do need to talk to you," Lauren stated as they both stood there quietly. "In my office."

"Right now?" said Sunny.

"Yes please." Lauren replied.

Sunny placed her things down and followed Lauren into her office where she was doing the same thing. Instead of grabbing her morning coffee, she noticed Lauren was packing up some things as if she was leaving.

"What's going on? You sounded so serious. Are you quitting?"

Lauren found that question to be funny. "What? No, I'm not quitting. Close the door behind you."

Sunny did as she was told and had a seat in a chair in front of Lauren's desk. "What is it that you wanted to talk about?"

"First let me say that you were right about someone following you. Ron's partner Mark was following you, but for good reasons."

"Ok, this is starting to sound a little creepy. Why was Mark following me? Do I need to get a restraining order on him?

"Sunny, no of course not. I had asked Ron to find out more information on Mr. Dewayne. Dewayne is not actually Dewayne. Apparently, his real name is Derrick. Dewayne is his twin brother."

"Identical twins?" Sunny asked as she scooted to the edge of her seat.

"Yeah, from the looks of it."

"Oh God, there's two of the arrogant boneheads. Please don't tell me we were dating them both?"

"No. Just Derrick. Who has a lengthy criminal rap sheet including a murder charge. He's been using his brother's name for a while. That's why when we went to his house, he acted like he didn't know us."

"Because he actually didn't know us. He was the real Dewayne. They look so much alike. He probably saw us as two crazy women," Sunny stated as she laughed.

"I know, but in the mean-time Ron wants us to stay away from both. So, I am going to be staying with Ron, and Mark will be nearby making sure you're ok."

"Wow, ok um…so that means Mark will be my personal body guard until this is over?"

"Yeah pretty much. He will be checking up on you."

"Have you spoken with Dale about everything?"

"No, I haven't. If I tell him it's possible that he will take me off the case and I can't have that. Not right now." Lauren began pacing the floor. Just the thought of being taken off the case bothered her. She's worked hard on this case. From late nights at the office, to bringing her work home have left her restless. To give up everything that she has worked on sounded like failure and failing wasn't an option.

"I know you're not going to like what I am about to say, but maybe it will be a good idea if we excused ourselves from the case."

"What? Are you out of your mind! Sunny I can't just take myself off the case. That would be like quitting and I'm not a quitter." Everything was too much for her right now. "Thanks again for the coffee," she stated as she took a sip.

"No problem. So, what do we do with this case?"

"We continue to work on it. We do whatever we need to do to complete it. The court date is in a few weeks. After that, then everything will be over."

"We can only hope," said Sunny.

"Exactly," Lauren replied. Just as she was about to take her seat, a knock came at the door. "Come in," she called out. Her door opened revealing her boss.

"Good morning ladies," he said as he stepped into Lauren's office.

"Dale… good morning. We were just discussing the case. It's coming along."

"The case is on hold until further notice."

"What do you mean it's on hold? We already have a court date in a few days."

"Cancel it or reschedule it. Evelyn is in the hospital," he stated as they both gasped at hearing those words.

"What happened? Lauren asked with great

sympathy.

"She was attacked in her home a few days ago. She was beaten badly," Dale said as he stood there with his head held down.

"Dale we're so sorry. If there's anything we can do please let us know," she said as she came to stand in front of him to show support. She knew how close the two of them were. This had to be hard for him.

"Thanks. The police think that it could be related to the case, but they are not for sure. Feel free to work on other cases until told otherwise. This case is now under a criminal investigation. I'll be in my office if you need me," he said before leaving out of Lauren's office.

As soon as he was gone, Lauren turned to look at Sunny. "What the fuck is going on?"

"I don't know, but whatever it is, I don't want to be next."

"You're not going to be next. Neither one of us will be next. So, don't talk like that. For all we know it could have been a random person."

"If you say so," Sunny replied as she got up from her seat. "Well, since we are officially off the case until further notice, I guess I should go file things away."

"The case isn't over. There's something going on and I am going to find out. I'm not throwing in the towel yet."

Sunny couldn't believe what she was hearing. She knew Lauren hated taking no for an answer, but this was getting out of hand. "Lauren are you crazy? You're not a detective. Leave that up to the pros. You're good at what you do here, but this is clearly out of your league."

"You're right."

"I am," said Sunny.

"Yeah, you're right."

"Wow! today is going to be a good day. This is like the second time ever that you agreed with me."

"I agree with you every day."

"I'm not talking about work. I'm talking about on a personal level," Sunny replied as she crossed her arms in front of her.

Lauren leaned against her desk and began thinking to herself. Now that her main case didn't require much of her attention, she might as well stay at work. She had plenty of other cases to get caught up on and complete. Maybe today would be a great day after all.

"Are you ok?" Sunny asked as she stared at Lauren who seemed to have zoned out for a minute.

"Yeah, just thinking about today. That's all," she said with a smile.

"Ok, well I am going to go file. If you need me I will be at my desk," said Sunny as she left out of Lauren's office.

Lauren stood there for a minute before taking a seat at her desk. She then pulled out her phone and began texting Ron, letting him know of everything that was going on and that she will be staying longer at work. She didn't go into full details. She hated explaining things in a text. Plus, she didn't want to hear him trying to change her mind.

She grabbed her briefcase and began pulling out the files from the case. She took one look at it before placing it aside to be filed, but something about it was calling her name. She had several files that needed her attention, but something about this one kept drawing her in. If she placed it aside to be filed, she knows that the daunting feeling of something is wrong will haunt her. She just had a few questions that she needed answered, then she could move on and call it a wrap.

She reached for the file and quickly opened it. She then read each paperwork like it was the first time. What was she missing? She had all the key elements she needed. She had to be overlooking something extremely important, but what was it? Then she saw it. How did she miss it? Is this why he wanted the file? She quickly gathered her things and left her office.

"Hey, you're early for lunch," Sunny said as she looked up from her computer.

"I need you to take my calls. I'm stepping out for a minute."

"Ok, yeah sure I can do that. Where are you going?"

Lauren hesitated for a minute before informing Sunny of where she was going. She was on a mission and didn't need anyone stopping her.

"I'm going to the hospital to see Evelyn," Lauren stated.

"What, are you serious? Are you crazy!" Sunny yelled.

"Shhh lower your voice."

"Are you crazy?" Sunny whispered.

"No, I'm not crazy. I need to find out what is going on. After this, I will close the door to this case. I promise."

"Does Dale know you're going?"

"No, he doesn't know. If he asks, just tell him I took an early lunch. I will be back soon," said Lauren before leaving.

CHAPTER SIXTEEN

Lauren arrived at The University Hospital minutes later. She quickly made her way in, stopping at the front desk to ask for directions before heading to the gift shop. She didn't want to come empty handed. After all, she did have a heart. Even for those who worked her nerves.

She took the elevator quietly to the third floor while carrying the get-well balloon and flower that she bought at the gift shop. The doors opened, and she stepped off. She then walked past the nurse's stations, following the numbers on the door until she reached Evelyn's room. She knocked lightly on the door. With no response, she knocked a littler harder the second time. The sound of Evelyn's voice telling her to come in was weak and somewhat sleepy.

"Hi Evelyn," Lauren said as she peeped her head

inside of the door before walking in.

"Lauren, hi. What are you doing here?" Evelyn replied.

"Well, I heard you were in here. So, I wanted to come by to see how you were doing?"

"How did you know I was here? Dale?"

"Yeah. Dale mentioned it to me," said Lauren. She tried not to stare but couldn't help to notice the bruises that covered her face, arms and her slightly swollen left eye. She was so caught up in everything that she had forgotten the gift she was holding. "Sorry, these are for you," she said as she set them on the nearest table beside the bed. "Don't know what I was thinking………I didn't mean to stare."

"It's ok. I was the same way when I looked at myself in the mirror."

"Did they catch the person that did this to you?" Lauren asked.

"Not that I am aware of. I haven't heard from anyone yet," Evelyn stated.

"Well…I'm sure they will catch the low life."

"Yeah, I hope so too. I didn't expect to see you. Why are you really here?" Evelyn asked as she coughed.

"I told you. I just wanted to see how you were doing?"

"Bullshit. You're not good at this. I hope you're a better lawyer than you are a liar."

"Ok well, the truth is I'm here to talk about your case. I'm not on the case anymore. Dale took me off, but something just wasn't sitting right with me. I need you to be honest with me," Lauren stated as she looked at Evelyn.

"Honest? You want me to be honest with you, when you are the one who came in here lying about your intentions."

"So, I lied. I'm sorry ok! but I'm not the only one lying here."

"What are you talking about?" Evelyn asked curiously.

"Don't fucking bullshit me. I know what you are up to." Lauren reached into her purse and pulled out the file she was working on and tossed it on the bed. "I had a very angry visit from someone. He was after the files. Now…I wondered why would he want the file? What could he possibly want with my file?"

"I don't know what you are talking about?" she said as she looked away from Lauren. Everything that she had planned was backfiring.

"Your husband didn't cheat on you, or did he?" Evelyn said nothing in return. She stared into blank space as if she was gathering her thoughts. "Look, I can help you and I really want to help you, but I just need to know the truth," said Lauren. She was beginning to lose her patience. "Say something!" Lauren yelled.

Evelyn looked at Lauren with tears in her eyes mixed with fear and frustration. "What do you want me to say!" she yelled as she wiped her tear stained cheeks, then looked away.

"The fucking truth! Whatever it is I promise… I will help you. Something is bothering you. I can tell. Please tell me……please, I promise we will get through this together."

Evelyn hesitated for a minute before turning to look at Lauren. She tried her best to hold in her tears but failed. The tears began pouring from her eyes as Lauren rushed to her side and had a seat on the edge of the bed.

"It's ok," said Lauren.

"I always thought my husband and I would be together until the end, but somewhere along the way things changed. He changed."

"How did he change?"

"He started working late. Some days he wouldn't come home. I suspected that he was sleeping around…I just couldn't catch him, but a woman knows when something isn't right," Evelyn said as she stared at Lauren. "I could smell the perfume on his clothes. I even found a number in his pocket. I called it and some woman answered it."

"What did she say?" Lauren asked.

"She stated that my husband was her man and that he was leaving me. She also stated that she was carrying his child. I confronted him and like always, he denied everything, but I knew he was lying. I was hurt and I wanted to see him hurt. I wanted sweet revenge. I didn't know what to do until one day he went out of town. The house phone rang, and it was a collect call from the Whiteville Correctional Facility."

"It was his brother," said Lauren.

"How did you know?"

"I did my homework," she stated. "What became of that phone call?"

"Well, I accepted the call. He wanted to speak to Dewayne, but I told him he was out of town. He then proceeded to tell me he was getting out of jail in two days and that he needed someone to pick him up. I told him I could pick him up and I did."

"What happened after you picked him up?"

"For starters, I was shocked to see that they were identical twins. When I looked at him, it was like looking at my husband. On the way back, we talked and talked. You know……he never knew about me. Dewayne never told his brother that he had gotten married."

"Maybe he just hadn't gotten around to do it."

"We've been married for almost five years Lauren, he had plenty of time," Evelyn stated.

"Yeah, that's true. So what else did the two of you talk about on the way back?"

"Nothing much. He told me some things about his brother that I didn't know about."

"What kind of things?"

"I made a promise that I wouldn't tell."

"Evelyn, I can't help you if you don't tell me everything. You gotta trust me. I'm not the enemy here."

"He told me that he wanted revenge on his brother. He didn't go into details, but I could tell that he was upset. Mostly because Dewayne never visited him while he was serving time and because they had a deal. He never mentioned what the deal was, but whatever it was, must have really pissed him off," Evelyn said as she coughed and cleared her throat. Lauren got up and poured her a cup of water.

"Here you go," Lauren said as she handed Evelyn the cup of water.

"Thank you," said Evelyn. "He did mention that he was framed."

"By who? His brother?"

"Yeah. So, afterwards, I put Derrick up in a hotel and told him to keep a low profile until everything was over."

"Everything like what? I'm lost here," said Lauren.

"I made a deal with him. If he can help me with my plan, I would make sure that he will get his share in the family business. He came up with hiring a private detective and capturing the photos to make it seem like he was having an affair. Dewayne and I, we had a prenup with stipulations."

"What kind of stipulations?" Lauren asked curiously as she waited for Evelyn's answer.

"I told him I would only sign a prenup, if he would remain faithful. If he cheats the prenup would be annulled. It would be as if it never existed."

"Why would Dewayne break into my place?"

Evelyn reached for the file that Lauren had tossed on the bed. She went through it until she landed on the fifth page, before handing it back to Lauren. "Read the small print," Evelyn stated. "My husband wanted his brother out of the picture."

Lauren took the paperwork and began reading it. She began asking herself how did she overlook this critical information? "Derrick owns fifty percent of the company."

"Does Dewayne even know his brother is out?" Lauren asked.

"I'm sure he does now," she said with a chuckle. "That's why he came to you. I found the papers in his office and took them. He found out and was upset. He threatened to kill me if I didn't tell him where it was……so I told him. I'm so sorry, I didn't know he would try to hurt you," Evelyn said apologetically.

"It's ok…...you didn't know."

"He could lose the company when we divorce. I get half of everything. I promised Derrick that I would take my half and sell it to him if he could help me get revenge. He eagerly accepted my offer."

"Giving him almost full ownership," Lauren stated.

"Exactly."

"You don't want to have stake in a high-powered company?" Lauren questioned.

"No. I don't want anything to do with him. He didn't love me. He only loved that company and I wanted him to know how it felt to lose something you love so much. He would kill for that company…." She was cut off by a knock at the door. "Come in," she called out.

"Hello Mrs. Price," the nurse said as she entered the room. Speaking to Lauren as well, she then placed a tiny cup down with a large pill in it on the table next to Evelyn.

Lauren tried not to be nosey, but it was in her nature to find out what was going on. She felt she only had part of the puzzle. There was still a lot to figure out, a lot until now.

"Here you go Mrs. Price," The nurse said as she

handed Evelyn the tiny cup with the pill in it. She then took the pitcher of water and refilled the cup Evelyn was holding.

Lauren wasn't crazy. She knew what kind of pill that was. The same kind her sister was taking, which was a prenatal. She may have the final piece to her puzzle. Lauren waited till the nurse was out of the room before she spoke again. "How far along are you?"

Evelyn didn't have anything else to hide. Everything was now out in the open and she felt that she could trust that Lauren would help her.

"Eleven weeks," Evelyn replied.

"Wow, congratulations."

"Thanks."

"You don't sound so happy about it," stated.

"I just wish the circumstances were different. There's so much that you don't know."

"So, was this the reason why you wanted to put a rush on things?"

Evelyn didn't say a word. She only shook her head in agreeance to the question that was asked.

"I can get Dale to put me back on the case. I'm sure everything will work out. Maybe. Not right away, but at least let's continue the process and ……"

"No!" Evelyn yelled. "Just let it be. You don't

know Dewayne like I know him. If he finds out he will make things bad for me. I just want to forget that any of this ever happened."

Lauren could see the hurt on her face. This wasn't the same Evelyn that came into her office demanding things. The woman before her was a woman that was hurt by love.

"I need to get back to work. It was nice seeing you Evelyn. If you need anything or have a change of heart, please don't hesitate to call," Lauren said before leaving out of the room.

She couldn't wait to tell Ron and Sunny of her findings, but who should she tell first? She knew that she couldn't tell her boss. He would probably scold her, seeing that he had already taken her off the case until matters were resolved. If she told Ron, he would probably be concerned about her safety and have men trailing her every move. So, that leaves Sunny, the only one that knew where she was, but wasn't overly concerned like Ron.

"Well, Sunny it is," she said to herself as she made her way out of the hospital and to the garage where her car was parked. She took her phone out of her purse and began dialing the office.

"Watson & Company Ms. Jones speaking, how can I help you?" Sunny answered.

"Sunny, you're not going to believe what I've found out."

"Hey, I was beginning to think you took the rest of the day off," Sunny jokingly stated.

"Of course not, but I have good news about the case."

"Well, technically its no longer your case, but carry on."

"Don't rain on my parade Sunny. I've come so close to solving this. Anyway, you're not going to believe this, but Evelyn is pregnant."

"Wait what?"

"She's pregnant."

"Ok, so she's possibly pregnant, big deal."

"No, she is pregnant. There's no possibly about it. I saw her taking a prenatal pill. Plus, she stated that she was pregnant. She didn't have anything to hide."

"Lauren what does this have to do with the case?"

"She didn't want her husband to find out. That's why she wanted the case expedited, but that's not the only thing. I will tell you the rest once I get back. You know...I somewhat feel sorry for her with everything she's going through."

"Seems like they have issues that you need to leave up to the detective to work out. I don't want to see you get hurt," said Sunny whom was greatly concerned.

"I'm not going to get hurt," she said as she made

it to her car. She opened her driver side door and threw her purse in the passenger seat before getting in. "Look, I really appreciate your concerns, but I am good."

"Just be careful and get back to work. Dale was asking about you a little while ago."

"Oh, gosh. What did you tell him?"

"I told him that you stepped out for an early lunch, but don't worry he stepped out as well.   Knowing him he will probably be gone all day."

"Great, you're such a lifesaver," Lauren said as she started her car. She locked her seatbelt in place before looking up in the mirror.

It all happened so fast as a hand reached out and grabbed her by her hair before placing a white cloth over her mouth and nose. She fought as hard as she could, but she was no match for the strength that the person possessed. She could hear Sunny on the phone as she felt herself drifting into a deep sleep. This is not how she pictured herself dying. She grabbed hold of the gear stick and shifted it to drive. She then slammed her foot on the pedal causing the car to take off. She was hoping to cause the person to lose balance, but it was too late. Her car slammed into another car as she tried her best to stay awake, but her eyes were too heavy. This time she couldn't wake up.

"Hello?" Sunny called out but there was no answer. "Hello? Lauren? Are you ok?" There was no sound of Lauren. The sound of the horn, blaring in the background was the only thing she could hear before the call went dead.

CHAPTER SEVENTEEN

Lauren slowly awoke, lying on the floor in the back seat of a white SUV. Her arms were tied behind her back, while her eyes and mouth were covered with tape. The last thing she remembered was getting into her car and someone attacking her from behind. Her head slightly hurt from crashing her car. Who was behind this? Most importantly where were they taking her? She was beginning to panic as she tried to free her hands, but the rope was too tight. The more she tried, the more she panicked. She began making noises as loud as she could. Maybe someone will hear her.

"Cut it out back there!" he yelled.

Lauren recognized the voice. It was either Dewayne or Derrick. Knowing what Dewayne was capable of, sent chills down her spine. Was this how she was going to die? By the hands of someone she thought she knew. Maybe she should have listened to Ron, he was right. She should have listened to him and stayed at the office. She needed him more than ever and if she lived to see another day, she would let him know exactly how she felt. Why was she thinking like this? She was a fighter and she will fight till the end. She began kicking the door as hard as she could, while still making as much noise as she could.

"Shut up bitch or else!" he yells angrily. "You brought this on yourself. All you had to do was give up the papers. I could have changed the names on it and slipped it back to you, but no. You turned my wife against me and set me up. You two were out to get me."

"You won't get away with this," she said through her muffled scream. She knew he didn't understand a word she was saying.

"Don't worry, lover boy won't find you. He's good, but he's not that damn good," he stated. "I should have known you were up to something when you came to my house. I should have taken care of you then, you and that other one with the big mouth, but don't worry. I will take care of her too."

Lauren continued her muffled screams as the tears began forming in her eyes. She should just give up, but she needed to stay strong for her friends and especially her family. She pulled herself together once again and began thinking of a plan. She could feel every bump and turn he made, but she still had no idea where she could be. The ride seemed like forever before the SUV came to a complete stop. She could hear the garage door opening.

She feared even more for her life. If anyone had seen them leaving the hospital, how could they identify the vehicle if it's hidden. Her thoughts were interrupted as she heard the door come open. She knew then she needed to give her all to get out alive. She started kicking and kicking but was no match for him.

"I should have roped those legs of yours, but I will enjoy them first," he said with a laugh.

She could feel where he was standing as she took her right foot and kicked him right where she knew it would hurt the most. The sound of Dewayne's voice filled the air from his hurt groin. She should run, but where would she run to? She remained on the floor and rested for a second. She had no where to run, but at least he won't be enjoying himself with her. At least not right now. She could still hear him groaning.

"You fucking bitch!"

She tried to listen carefully on what he might be doing. She needed to prepare herself for whatever might happen next. All she could hear were tools or something clanking together, as if he was searching for something. Minutes later she felt her feet being tied together.

"Try kicking out of this," he said between his teeth. He then grabbed her and tossed her over his shoulder and carried her inside. He didn't stop until he reached his destination, a queen size bed where he dropped her down with force.

Lauren cried as she felt him straddle her body

before placing a hand around her neck. He then quickly removed the taped.

"Ahh!" she screamed from the pain of the tape being ripped away.

"You scream and I will kill you right here," he demanded.

"You don't have to do this," she cried. "Whatever you want. I can get it for you."

"Don't you think it's a little too late for that now? There's nothing you can give me now. You have destroyed everything that mattered to me. My wife, my job and my future."

"Don't do this! Just let me help," she cried. "Please, let me go."

"I can't do that."

"Yes you can. Just…"

"No I can't!" he yelled. "You know too much already. I know that you know and because of that, I can't let you go. You see, I was there at the hospital. I know you made a visit to Evelyn."

"She didn't tell me anything."

"You know, you're not a good liar."

"You won't get away with this. They will catch you. He will catch you."

"They didn't catch me the first time. That's the good thing about having a twin," he said right as a knock came to the door. Followed by the doorbell. "Fuck."

Lauren took this moment to try and yell, but was cut off by Dewayne's hand covering her mouth, as something sharp and pointed touched her neck.

"You scream, I promise I will kill you," he said before placing the tape back across her mouth. He then grabbed her and moved her again.

All Lauren could hear was the doorbell, ringing chaotically as the person pounded on the door before being tossed aside into a smaller room. From the smell of everything, she assumed she was in a closet of all places. Better there than in a lake. Whoever stopped by just bought her more time. Hopefully Sunny will get in touch with Ron. He'll know what to do.

She could now hear another male voice in the house. She should scream but was too scared to do so. They were arguing. Were they arguing over her? Or was he there to finish her? She's only been gone for a short amount of time, but it seemed like forever.

She tried to put her mind at ease in hopes that Ron was near but couldn't help but notice the commotion that was taking place nearby in another room. She could tell glass was being broken and things were being thrown. What was going on? She needed Ron more than she had ever needed anyone ever. She just needed to keep fighting to stay alive. He's come, she just knew that he would. Next time she will listen......if there's ever a next time.

,

CHAPTER EIGHTEEN

Sunny paced the bathroom floor as she tried to figure out what was going on. "Think, think, think," she said to herself. The last thing she heard was a muffled scream coming from Lauren and the sound of the horn before the call went dead. She grabbed her cellphone out of her pocket and began calling Lauren again, but it went straight to voicemail. "Shit, where are you? Lauren answer the phone. I need to know you're ok. Call me back or else!" she pleaded into the voicemail as a knock came on the door.

She locked it, so she could have a moment to herself. She didn't want anyone to over hear what was going on. She didn't know what was going on, but she needed to find out. She stared at herself in the mirror, wondering what in the hell she has gotten herself into. Maybe she should have talked Lauren into not going. It was now do or die time. If she was in Lauren's situation, she knew what Lauren would do. A knock came at the door again, breaking her thoughts and concentration. She took a deep breath and a moment to calm her nerves before opening the restroom door.

"Sorry," she said to her coworker before leaving out. "It's all yours." She tried to force a smile, but the situation wouldn't let her. She hurried away from the restroom stopping by Lauren's office, hoping for a miracle but there was no sign of her. "Dammit Lauren!" she yelled quietly to herself. She reached her desk and pulled her cellphone from out of her pocket, and still no calls or texts from Lauren. She picked up her work phone and began calling her from it, again no word from her. It went straight to voicemail. This was making her furious, anxious, nervous and scared.

"Hey Cheryl," she said to her co worker sitting near her. "I'm going to take an early lunch. Do you mind covering the phones?"

"No go ahead," she replied.

"Thanks, you're a lifesaver. I owe you," Sunny said as she grabbed her things and was about to head out the door.

"Well since you said it, do you think you can pick me up a burger on your way back? If you don't mind," Cheryl asked.

Sunny stopped and closed her eyes. She didn't think her co worker would take her up on that offer so soon. "Umm, yeah sure."

"Thanks!" Cheryl said as she began going through her purse looking for her wallet.

Either she was slow or Sunny was just in too much of a hurry, but she didn't have time for her co worker to sit there and go through countless amounts of change.

"You know what, I am in a hurry. You can just pay me back later," said Sunny as she turned around and began to leave.

"Are you sure?"

"Yep," Sunny replied as she threw up her right hand. She walked as fast as she could through the main hallway and out the door. She prayed she wasn't too late. Every minute wasted was a chance she would never see her friend again. She reached into her purse and grabbed her phone. When she looked up, the situation changed for either better or worse. "Shit!" she said to herself. She tried to calm her nerves before hell breaks loose…...again. "Mark, hey what are you doing here? I thought Lauren mentioned that we didn't need any security," she said nervously. "We're capable of taking care of ourselves."

"Well, I came to check on you two anyway. It's my job. Why are you outside? The two of you were supposed to stay in. I'm glad someone is paying attention."

"How sweet of you, but…well actually she

umm…she's not here."

"What do you mean she's not here? She was supposed to stay inside, both of you," said Mark.

Sunny could tell that he was getting upset. Which made her scared to tell him what was really going on. But really, deep down inside she had no choice. She hoped Lauren didn't hate her for what she was about to do. If Ron found out he would be highly upset.

"The truth is…she left to go to the hospital."

"The hospital? What's wrong with her? Is she ok?" he asked.

"No! I mean, I hope. I mean she was ok when she left. She went to see Evelyn."

"What do you mean she was ok when she left? Did something happen to her?"

"I don't know. That's what I'm hoping to find out. She called me as she was leaving the hospital. One minute we were talking and the next minute I hear a muffled scream before the call went dead."

"Fuck!" Mark yelled. "This is why you were supposed to stay inside!"

"Sorry."

"Sorry can't fix this," he replied. "Have you heard from her?"

"I've been trying to call her ever since, but I can't

reach her. Her phone is off," Sunny stated as she looked down towards the ground. "I was on my way to the hospital. She's probably still there."

Mark didn't say anything. The look he gave Sunny showed her that he was extremely pissed off right about now. If he could only say what he really wanted to say to her right now he would, but his mind was on explaining to Ron the situation with Lauren. He immediately took his phone out of his pants pocket and began calling Ron.

Sunny said nothing as she watched Mark have a heated discussion with Ron, who sounded pissed off. She could hear the conversation. Nothing about it sounded happy. She was almost in tears but needed to stay strong for Lauren.

After ending the call, he turned to walk away.

"Where are you going?" she asked as she held back her tears.

"I'm going to find Lauren. Go back inside. Ron and I will handle this."

"What? No! I'm going with you," Sunny demanded.

"You're not going with me. It's no place for someone like you," he stated as he looked her up and down. Her gray semi mini skirt hugged her body, as the white fitted shirt hugged her breasts. Not to mention the way her legs looked in the four- inch black heels.

"What is that supposed to mean? Someone like

me?" she said offensively.

Mark took a deep breath and ran his hands down his face. Today was not going the way he hoped. "Look, I don't need anyone slowing me down. You're not going."

"I'm going and that's the end of this conversation. The longer we stand here and discuss this the longer my friend is still in danger. Now, if we take the highway, we can be at the hospital in no time," she said as she walked past him and headed towards his black SUV. Since they were going in the same direction, she figured that she might as well join him, instead of driving her car.

Mark didn't want to argue with Sunny. He knew this was one fight he wouldn't win, but she was right about one thing. The longer they stood there, the shorter their chances were at finding Lauren alive.

Sunny wasted no time as she opened the door to Mark's SUV and got inside. Mark hurried to the driver side and got in as well then drove off. Neither spoke on their way to the hospital. For a few minutes the ride was quiet until the sound of Mark's phone interrupted the silence.

"Yeah, talk to me," he said to the caller. The call seemed to go on forever, leaving Sunny in suspense as she waited for answers. "I will meet you there," he said before hanging up.

"Who was that?" she asked in fear. She didn't mean to pry into his personal conversation, but right now she didn't care.

"That was Ron. Looks like a change of plan." He stated.

"What kind of change of plan?" Sunny asked.

"Lauren's phone was turned back on. He was able to track it to a house not far from here."

"Oh God I hope she's ok. She has to be ok," said Sunny as the tears began forming in her eyes. She tried her best to hold them back but couldn't. She gave in as her tears began filling her eyes, staining her cheeks as they fell. Just thinking about Lauren made her tears fall harder.

"Don't cry," said Mark softly.

"I can't help it. I should have talked her out of it, but I covered for her instead. It's my fault," she sobbed.

"It's not your fault," he said as he grabbed her hand. "Stop beating yourself up. Everything will be ok I promise. You're too beautiful to be crying." He meant every word that he said, even the part about Sunny being beautiful. He wondered how it would be to feel her under him. He could fall in love with her, but he knew he wasn't her type. She was probably used to men in expensive suits. Not some guy in jeans and a t-shirt. He quickly snapped out of his thoughts and released her hand. He then grabbed a Kleenex from the arm rest and handed it to her. "Here you go."

"Thank you," she said as she tried to force a smile. She took the Kleenex and wiped her eyes as she tried not to ruin her makeup anymore than she already did. She stared out the window as her thoughts consumed her. Her mind went to the moment he held her hand. He was gentle. Even though she was crying and upset, she felt a sense of relief when he held her hand. She wondered what kind of husband he would make. Could he be faithful? Was she even his type? She was getting ahead of herself.

"We're coming up on the house," he said.

Sunny instantly recognized the area. She knew where they were headed. "I know this area. We've been here before."

"What are you talking about?" Mark asked.

"A few days ago, we paid him a visit. He almost called the cops on me, but I left."

"Who are you talking about?"

"This Dewayne guy we supposedly had dated. I came to his house to confront him for being a jerk. When I got there,

he acted like he didn't know me. Lauren went there as well, and he acted the same way. To make a long story short he wasn't even the right guy. He was the brother."

Mark looked over at Sunny. "Women," he said under his breath.

"What was that?" she asked quickly.

"Nothing," he replied. He didn't want to get into

another discussion. They had more important things to deal with. "Looks like Ron is already here. I will need for you to stay inside."

"What? Are you kidding me!" Sunny yelled.

"No, I'm not kidding. You don't know what you're getting yourself into," he said as he parked his SUV behind Ron's SUV.

"The same goes for you as well," Sunny stated.

"Yeah but I am more capable of taking care of the situation than you are." He unbuckled his seatbelt and opened his door.

"And?"

"And you're not getting out. Stay inside."

"You're not my man. You can't tell me what to do!" she yelled as he got out and closed the door. She crossed both arms in front of her, she was fuming. She doesn't take orders from anyone that doesn't sign her check. Even though he was right, she couldn't just sit there and do nothing.

CHAPTER NINTEEN

Ron sat in his SUV as he watched Mark exit his vehicle. He grabbed his gun from the glove compartment. He then placed it in the holder on his waist, pulling his shirt down over it before exiting his vehicle.

"Thanks for coming," Ron said to Mark.

"No problem. So, what's the plan?"

"There is no plan. The cops are on the way."

"So, we're waiting for the cops to get here?" Mark asked.

"Hell no! I'm going to get my woman. I'm not going to sit around and wait for something to happen. If he touches a single hair on her head, he's dead," Ron said angrily which showed on his face. The audacity of anyone putting their hand on Lauren, pissed him off. He knew she was more than capable of taking of herself, but he felt it was his job to protect her. She was his and even though she didn't know it yet, he planned to make sure she knew it, when everything was over.

"So, this Dewayne guy what else did you find out about him?" Mark asked.

"Not much. The company that he now owns belonged to his father. When his father died, majority of the company was left to his brother. After his brother went away, he took over. Now that his brother is back, all I can think of is he would do anything to keep it."

"Even kill?"

"Even kill," Ron replied.

"Well, what are we waiting on?" Mark asked as he took his gun out of the holder and checked it before placing it back into the holder on his side. "You ready to go get your girl?"

"Ready as…." Ever was what he was going to say, but was distracted when he saw a familiar face exit Marks SUV. "What the fuck is she doing here?"

Mark turned to look at his SUV. "Fuck," he said as he threw both hands up. "She wouldn't take no for an answer." Sunny was exiting the SUV and walking their way. He clearly told her to stay inside. Apparently, she had a hearing problem.

"You need to handle your girlfriend," Ron stated.

"She's not my girlfriend. Never have and never will be. She doesn't listen."

"That's all women," Ron replied right as Sunny was walking up.

"Hey, so what's the plan?" she said right away.

"The plan was for you to stay inside," Mark stated.

"We've already discussed this. I'm not going to sit around and do nothing while my friend is in harm's way."

"Look, you two love birds can argue later," Ron said as he intervened. He didn't have time to babysit. He left the two standing there. The love of his life needed him and every second counted.

"Ok, so what do I need to do?" Sunny asked.

"Are you fucking serious right now?" Mark replied as he too started walking towards the house, trailing Ron.

"I just want to help and I'm not taking NO for an answer," she called out as she began following Mark. "How many times do I have to say that? My answer won't change."

Ron was already at the front door with his gun drawn. He knocked as hard and loud as he could. He didn't care who was there. He knocked again, this time even louder and still no answer.

"I'm kicking the door in," Ron said impatiently. He didn't care about not having a warrant. He will deal with the consequences later. He looked at Mark, giving him the signal to cover him before kicking open the door. Broken glass was everywhere, and furniture was tossed around. There was clearly a struggle here, which made him even more angry. "Lauren!" he immediately called out. "Lauren!"

"Lauren!" Sunny yelled out as well causing Ron to look over at Mark.

"Don't ask," Mark whispered.

Sunny began carefully following behind Mark. All while thinking how she should have listened to him. He was right all along. This was no place for her. She had no training whatsoever and the only thing she was good at, was running. They continued searching each room, but there was no sign of Lauren. Her heart beat against her chest as they made their way around towards the kitchen.

Sunny gasped at the sight before her. "Oh my goodness," she said as she pointed towards the blood stains on the kitchen floor.

"Go wait in the truck," Mark suggested.

This time she listened. "Ok," was all she said as she turned and left.

"The trail of blood leads……it leads to the garage," said Mark.

"I swear if he hurt her in anyway……he's a dead

man," Ron said furiously.

Mark opened the door to the garage and looked inside. "It's empty." Just as he was about to close the door, they heard a scream coming from the front of the house. They both looked at each other before heading in that direction. They just knew it was Lauren. Sunny was out of the house. It had to be her.

As they entered the front room, they saw Dewayne pulling Sunny from the front door with his arm around her neck.

"Get your damn hands off of her!" Mark yelled. This was the main reason why he wanted her to stay behind at the office. Right now, he was full of emotions, pissed off and concerned. Even though him and Sunny had their exchange of words, it would kill him if anything happened to her.

Dewayne turned around with a knife to Sunny's neck. The anger in his eyes showed, along with the blood on his jeans and white shirt. "You all just couldn't leave me alone."

"Just drop the knife, let her go and tell us where Lauren is," said Mark.

"I've worked hard for everything that I have and now, you all are trying to take it all away. My job, my wife…everything!"

"No one is trying to take anything away from you. Just let her go and tell us where Lauren is. We know she's here," Ron stated. "Her phone shows her here, in your place."

"That doesn't mean a damn thing," he laughed.

Ron took a step closer, causing Dewayne to press the knife closer to Sunny's neck.

"Stay back!" Dewayne yelled.

"You don't have to do this. Let her go!" yelled Ron. "Just let her go and we both win."

"No……I win," Dewayne said while pointing his knife at Mark and Ron.

"If you kill her, you will never get away with it," Mark stated.

Hearing those words made Dewayne smile. "I've done it before and I'm sure I could do it again." Just as he began to place the knife at Sunny's neck, Mark fired his gun. Hitting Dewayne in the right shoulder, causing him to instantly loosen his grip on Sunny and dropping the knife.

At that moment Sunny ran as quick as she could into Mark's arms that welcomed her. "I'm sorry," she cried.

"It's ok," he replied.

Dewayne was now on the floor holding his arm as Ron came closer with his gun, pointing it directly at him before kicking the knife out of reach. He wanted to finish him. He wanted him to hurt just like he was hurting, not knowing if Lauren was ok or not.

"Where is she?" Ron demanded. "Where in the fuck is she!" Ron could hear the sirens outside.

"As I was leaving, I thought I heard something coming from there," Sunny said as she pointed towards a door that was cracked open. "I never got chance to check it out because this asshole attached me."

"Go check it out," said Mark and he held Sunny in one arm and the gun in the other hand pointing directly at Dewayne. "I'll stay here and watch him until the cops take him. Go find Lauren."

That was all the confirmation that Ron needed. He knew Mark would take care of everything. Sunny was in good hands and soon Lauren will be safe in his.

He waisted no time as he headed in the direction that Sunny pointed. He rushed towards the cracked door and pushed it open. "Lauren!" he called out but there was no answer. He yelled again this time louder. "Lauren! I'm here. Where are you?" He listened closely, hoping to hear some sign of her and he did.

The muffled sound of Lauren's voice came from a closet. Followed by a slight thump against the wall. She was trying to let him know where she was.

Ron kept calling her name as he opened the closet door. There against the wall was Lauren with her hands tied behind her, blindfolded and her mouth gagged. Just the thought of seeing her like that sent rage throughout his body. He quickly scooped her up into his arm and carried her out of the closet where he could better examine her. He began taking off her blindfold. Her brown eyes that once showed love, now showed fear. He then proceeded to remove the remaining objects that bounded her.

Lauren was excited and felt a world of relief as Ron held her in his arms. "I'm so sorry," she cried. "I should have stayed at the office."

For a minute, Ron couldn't say anything. He just wanted to hold her and make sure she was ok. "Are you ok?" he asked.

"Yeah…I'm ok. Just a little shaken up, but I'm ok," she replied.

"Did he hurt you? Because if he did, I swear to God he will……"

"He didn't hurt me," she immediately replied as she placed both hands on the side of his face and gave him a kiss. "I'm ok, but I don't know what would have happened if you hadn't showed up."

"Me either and I don't want to think about it. You're safe now and I promise I will never let anything happen to you again. How about we get you out of here?"

"Ok," she replied as Ron helped her off the floor.

"You're limping?" he asked.

"Yeah I think I hurt my ankle when I was kicking."

They made their way into the front room were the others were waiting.

"Lauren!" Sunny screamed as she left Mark's side to give her a big hug. "I'm so happy you're ok. I should have talked you out of not going."

"You of all people should know that wouldn't have worked," Lauren replied. Lauren then looked at Dewayne. "So, it's you. You are the one who was following me a few days ago."

"What are you talking about?" Ron asked.

"A few days ago, when I was leaving home, I thought I saw someone following me."

"Why didn't you tell me?" he asked.

"I wasn't for sure. I didn't want to make a big deal out of something I just wasn't so sure about. Now that I see the scar on his face, I'm even now sure that it was him."

Ron turned his attention to Dewayne sitting on the floor, still holding his shoulder from the gunshot wound. He pulls the gun from its holder and placed it to Dewayne's head. "I should kill you right here," he said angrily. "I should blow your fucking brains out!" he yelled.

"Do it," Dewayne said as he laughed. "I'm as good as dead. "I've already lost everything. Do it. Do it!" he screams.

"My pleasure," Ron stated as he took the safety off.

"Wait!" Lauren called out. "Don't kill him. He will have a bigger responsibility to deal with in a few months. Plus, I need you here with me and not behind bars."

"This beautiful lady here just saved your undeserving ungrateful ass," he stated before lowering his gun from Dewayne's head. "Must be your lucky day."

Lauren made her way to Ron's side. "If you ever put your hands on me again, next time I won't be so nice," she said before giving Dewayne a blow to the side of his face with her fist.

Ron smiled at the sight of Lauren. He couldn't help but to admire the women in front of him. The woman that he fell in love with. Even though he said he would never fall in love but somehow, she came along and changed his mind. She left her handprint in his heart and he couldn't wait to tell her just how much she means to him.

CHAPTER TWENTY

The Next Day

Lauren laid stretched out in bed. A bed that was unfamiliar to her. A bed she never knew before but was enjoying the comfort of it now. After a crazy day and a long week ahead, laying next to Ron was what she needed. She felt safe whenever she was around him. She finally felt like she found the one, but only time will tell. She needed to hear those words from his mouth, letting her know how he really felt.

She looked around the room, it was nice but, could use a woman's touch. Maybe her touch. If Ron found out she was thinking of adding a woman's touch to his room, he would probably flip out. Which could probably push him away. What was she thinking? Lauren sat up in bed as she saw Ron walk into the bedroom carrying a tray loaded with breakfast. For a second, she admired his physique. From the white t-shirt that hugged his muscles, to the gray sweat pants that she loved so much. Only because they gave her a sneak peak of what's to come.

"Good morning beautiful," he said as he came and stood next to her. He placed the tray on the nightstand before sitting on her side of the bed.

"Good morning. I was wondering where you went off to," she replied.

"I wanted to treat you to breakfast in bed. You've been through a lot."

"Thanks, you shouldn't have."

"It's the least I can do. Since I wasn't there to protect you," he said as he took hold of her hands.

"It wasn't your fault. I should have listened."

The words that were coming next wasn't something he had to think about. He knew from the moment he met Lauren this was what he wanted. "I want you to move in with me."

"Ron." Lauren didn't want to go there. How could he talk about moving in when he hasn't said the words she wanted to hear? She needed more than a I love you statement. She needed to know where they stood with each other.

"Hear me out. You are home alone a most of the time. What if something happens? What if this creep comes back?"

"He won't come back. He's in jail. There's nothing he can do from jail," said Lauren.

"He can do a lot from jail if he knows the right people. I've already lost you once and I don't want that to happen again."

Lauren was lost for words. The look in his eyes were sincere. She felt every word he was saying, but she needed more to give a definite answer. "Ron…I don't know. How about we just enjoy the day for now," she replied as she gave him a sweet kiss on the lips, but he wanted more.

"Ok, I can work with that answer as long as you promise to take it into consideration."

"I promise I will take it into consideration."

"Is it too early for dessert?" Ron removed his white t-shirt before throwing the sheets off Lauren's body.

"It's never too early for dessert," she said as she blushed. She watched his sculptured body as he laid between her legs. Still wearing his gray sweats, she could feel the outline of him, which made her aroused and ready.

He kissed her lips softly with passion. He wanted to devour them, but right now he needed to be gentle. He had plenty of time to have his way with her. "You know, there's something I need to tell you," he said between kisses. "Something I haven't said to another woman."

"Do you hear that?" she replied. She wanted to focus on him but couldn't help to notice the noise coming from downstairs.

"No, I don't hear anything." He began kissing her neck as his hand massaged her breast.

She really wanted to focus, but he was making it extremely hard. That and the disturbance still coming from downstairs. "Ron, I think someone one is knocking."

He gave her one last kiss before getting up and putting his shirt back on. He then checked the security system on his phone. "It's Mark and Sunny."

"What?" she asked as she grabbed a shirt dress from out of her overnight bag. She then went to the bathroom to freshen up and dress. "I wonder what they are doing here so early." She returned fully dressed.

He undressed her with his eyes. "I don't know, but I do know that ass is mine after they leave," he stated. He couldn't stop looking at her. Even in the simplest things, she still looked amazing. "You ready?"

"Yeah. I'm ready." She followed him downstairs and had a seat on the sofa, while Ron answered the door. She could hear Sunny's voice as soon as the door opened.

"Lauren!" Sunny called out. "Lauren, oh my goodness. How are you?"

"I'm good. How are you with everything?" Lauren asked. "Are you taking an early lunch break?"

"Well, actually I took the day off. I needed a short break."

"You deserved it. You've been working as hard as me on this case," said Lauren. "You were right there with me, every step of the way."

"Literally!" Mark shouted as he entered the room. "You could have gotten us killed."

"But did you die?" Sunny stated.

"What does that have to do with anything," he replied as he shook his head.

"He's still yapping about yesterday," Sunny said as she rolled her eyes at him.

"Yapping? I will remember that the next time you need my help," said Mark.

"You guys would make the perfect couple," said Lauren with a smile.

"I don't think so. He's too bossy," Sunny replied.

"Bossy?"

"Anyway. What are you two doing here? You interrupted our love session," said Ron.

"I just wanted you to know that I got word that Evelyn still wants us to represent her."

"That means, Dale has assigned us back on the case!" Lauren asked with joy.

"Yep. We make one great team I must say."

"That we do. I'm also glad Evelyn decided to go ahead with the divorce. No one should stay where they are not happy. Plus, she has a little person to think about now." Thinking of Evelyn made her think about her own sister and the new bundle of joy that will soon arrive.

Ron couldn't help but to smile at the joy he saw on Lauren's face. He wanted to do everything within his power to make sure it stayed there, but he also couldn't help but to notice the puzzled look that was now on her face.

"What's wrong?" he asked as he went to sit beside her. He grabbed her hand to reassure her that, whatever it is everything would be ok.

"I was just curious about what happened to Derrick? Where is he?"

"No one has heard from him," Mark stated as he looked at Ron. He then took a seat in a chair near Sunny. "I checked every source that we have and each time I've come up empty handed."

"You don't think something happened to him?" Lauren asked.

"I don't know, but when he held a knife to Sunny's neck, we thought it was your blood."

"What? No, it wasn't my blood. At least not that much."

"Well, if it wasn't yours then who's was it?" Sunny questioned.

Ron knew it was a possibility that it was Derrick's blood, but he didn't want her to worry. After things have died down, he would fill her in what's going on. "I guess that's something that the police and detective will need to figure out," said Ron. He needed to intervene. He didn't want Lauren playing detective just to ease her curiosity. "You just need to focus on getting better and spending time with me." He pulled Lauren close and gave her a promising kiss. For a second, they almost forgot that they had company.

Mark then turned to Sunny. He came to her rescue. He deserved some appreciation too and Sunny had a feeling he was thinking exactly that.

"Don't even think about it?" said Sunny. "Do we need to go? Because it looks like your friend here is getting ideas," she said as she pointed to Mark.

"As a matter of fact, I think that would be a great idea," Ron stated as he stood up. "I need to finish showing this awesome woman here of mine just how much I love her."

Sunny smiled as she got up from her seat. "Aww, well on that note, I guess we will get going," she said.

"Thank you for stopping by and checking on me.

I promise I will keep you posted on my return to work." They gave each other a hug, while Mark and Ron finished up their conversation.

"Let's go Mark. These two need their privacy," Sunny called out.

"Wait, you two rode together?" Lauren asked.

"Yes, talk to your boss about my raise so that this," she stated as she pointed to herself and Mark, "doesn't happen again."

Lauren laughed at Sunny's comment before waving them both out the door. "Those two are like oil and water."

"I think they are capable of loving each other one day. They just need to get to know each other more."

"You think so?"

"Yeah, I really do."

"Well, speaking of love. Did you mean what you said about how much you love me?"

Ron pulled Lauren into his arms and looked her directly in the eyes. He wanted her to know that every word that was about to come out of his mouth is true.

"Yeah, it's true. I love you Lauren Hamilton. I think I loved you from the first time I ever laid eyes on you."

She was happy to hear those words and even

happier that she could say them back. "I love you too Ron. I know we have our ups and downs and I'm not the easiest to deal with."

"It's ok. That doesn't stop me from wanting you and loving you. Plus, I'm not the easiest to deal with either. I want you, all of you. The good and the bad. I still want you here with me. If you want to find another place together, I'm open to that as well.

Lauren was all smiles. Her heart was full of love, that she didn't know could have existed. "Ok."

"Ok to what?"

"Ok to us. I don't want to get married no time soon, but I do want to see where love takes us. As far as me moving in, let's just finish what we started earlier. Maybe you can change my mind. In the meantime, I'm all yours."

Ron scooped Lauren up in his arms and carried her to his bed, where he placed her down. He took his previous position between her legs as they kissed passionately. He couldn't wait to finish what he started. He wanted nothing more than to claim what was finally his.

"You should have been mine all along," he stated in between kissing.

Lauren was about to say something but was thrown off when she felt Ron at her entrance. She's loved before, but nothing like this. He was everything and some. She should have trusted her heart a long time ago. As of now, he was hers and she was his and that was all that mattered. She was made for him and he was made for her and by the time he was finished with her, they will both know just who they belong to.